DIAL L FOR LOVE

After I'd said goodbye to Hank and hung up the phone, I sat and stared into space for a while. Funny, I thought, how you can judge a person to be one way, and then he turns out to be completely different. Hank had seemed so quiet and shy, and yet by digging a little under the surface, I'd discovered that he had a sense of humor and a way of looking at things that made me suspect we had a lot in common.

First impressions are deceiving, I thought.

Aren't they?

Dial
L for Love

Marian Woodruff

BANTAM BOOKS
TORONTO · NEW YORK · LONDON · SYDNEY

RL 5, IL age 11 and up

DIAL L FOR LOVE
A Bantam Book/October 1983
Reprinted 1985

Cover photo by Pat Hill.

ISBN 0 553 17072 4

Published simultaneously in the United States and Canada

*Bantam Books are published by Bantam Books, Inc. Its trademark,
consisting of the words "Bantam Book" and the portrayal of a rooster,
is Registered in U.S. Patent and Trademark Office and in other countries.
Marca Registrada. Bantam Books, Inc., 666 Fifth Avenue, New York,
New York 10103.*

Printed and bound in Great Britain by
Anchor Brendon Ltd, Tiptree, Essex

O 0 9 8 7 6 5 4 3 2 1

*To Susan, who never lets me forget
what best friends are for.*

*With acknowledgment to Karen Felts
of Jazzercise for her kind assistance.*

Dial
L for Love

Chapter One

"Hey, Mattie, I think he likes you," whispered Linda, jabbing me with her elbow as Hank Butterfield skated past the hockeyrink bleachers.

I gaped in amazement at my best friend, Linda Franklin. "You're nuts! Hank's never spoken two words to me. I'd probably faint if he even asked me for the time of day. What gives you the idea he *likes* me?"

Linda smiled mysteriously. Everything she does has a mysterious air to it—so I should know better than to be surprised at anything she thinks. Since the age of ten, when we

1

became friends, she's been planning on being the next Agatha Christie. She's written about half a dozen mystery novels—all unpublished—and has a mind even Nancy Drew would envy. When we were ten, a missing skate key became *The Case of the Purloined Key.* Now that we're sixteen, her overactive imagination is busy exploring fresh, uncharted territory; namely, boys.

"Didn't you see the way he *looked* at you just now?" she persisted, her brown eyes narrowing in a knowing squint.

"He was probably looking at the scoreboard. Another slap shot like that last one and he'll be riding home on the team's shoulders."

"I see the feeling isn't one-sided," she said, smirking.

"Will you get off it? Hank doesn't even know I'm alive."

"How can you say that when he's only two seats away from you in government?" she asked. "The only thing between you and Hank Butterfield is Janine Hawes."

I sighed. "With Janine around, I might as well be part of the blackboard."

Even so, I had to admit that Janine—the

shapely brunette temptress of our junior class at Port Kearney High—had failed to score with Hank as far as I could see. Out of the corner of my eye, I'd been watching the way she would drape herself over Hank's desk, fluttering her long eyelashes at him while asking something utterly inane like should she cut her hair or let it grow long, or did he think the color of her dress matched her eyes? As if the entire future of the world depended on his answer. Ugh! I can't believe it when girls act that way. I mean, flirting is fine, but a little bit goes a long way as far as I'm concerned.

Besides, I'm not really the flirty type, if you're going strictly by looks, that is. What I mean is, compared to Janine I'm fairly ordinary-looking. When we sculpted self-portraits in art class, I was tempted to make my nose a little thinner and my mouth a little less wide. I didn't have to worry about my freckles though—there was no way of making them show up on clay, for which I was grateful.

My one outstanding feature, if it can be called that, is my hair, which is full and practically waist-length, blond with streaks of gold mixed in. Ever since grade school, kids have been teasing me about it—in a nice way—like in sixth grade when I was nicknamed Golden Girl for the entire year.

"Maybe he's the shy type," suggested Linda.

"Maybe." I shrugged. "To tell the truth, I haven't given it that much thought." Hank, the resident superjock of Port Kearney High, was tall, sandy-haired and handsome, so I supposed he could have his pick of almost any girl at school.

What's more, he was the star of our ice hockey team at school, which is about the most exciting thing Port Kearney, Washington, has to offer in the wintertime. In January we're always buried up to our ears in snow.

Our team, the Port Kearney Kannonballs, had just scored a goal, thanks to Hank and a magnificent backhand slap shot, into the corner of the net, boosting the score in the final minutes of the game to a nerve-racking five to five. As Hank glided across the ice, I could see the tension stamped on his weather-reddened face. With Linda's words still echoing in my mind, I did a double take, concentrating on the way the dampness had sent his blond hair spiraling into ringlets—he certainly *was* handsome. But the only thing on his mind, I was sure, was sliding the puck into that net one more time.

Linda clutched my arm as the puck shot past a defenseman and was captured by our center, Bud Steward, a tall, red-haired boy with arms like pistons. Bud darted into an opening, head bent and skates flying as he hurtled down the ice toward a net that suddenly seemed a million miles away. Our frantic cheers punctuated the chill air with plumes of vapor, spurring him on as he sent the puck whizzing home—only to be blocked by the Eagles' goalie, a short, sleepy-looking boy who could come to life instantly when necessary.

There was a loud crack as the black rubber puck shot back over the ice in the direction it had come, a stream of players in hot pursuit. The kids in the bleachers on both sides were going crazy, screaming and hollering at full pitch. In front of me, petite ladylike Sue Vallone vaulted up on tiptoe, waved a red mitten, and yelled, "Nail 'em, Hank!"

The puck neared the boards, with two players, Hank versus the Eagles' center, closing in from either side. Hank's stick flashed a split second before that of his opponent,

5

and the puck skipped over to our defenseman, Jamie Lyons. Bravely Jamie lunged into a forest of thrashing sticks; then suddenly he was flying head over heels, landing with a horrible thud against the boards. The referee's whistle shrilled, calling for a penalty against the Eagles. Jamie was OK, as it turned out, but he was limping as the coach helped him off the ice.

Linda jabbed a mittened finger in the direction of the bench. "Look who they're sending in to replace Jamie. Isn't that Jay Thompson?"

He looked vaguely familiar, then I remembered that I'd seen him hanging around with Hank. Jay was shorter than Hank, more wiry than muscular, with dark hair that dipped over a pair of cinnamon-brown eyes. He had a wide mouth, which was now set in a thin line of determination.

The game had gone into sudden-death overtime. Jay skated over to fill in Jamie's empty right wing spot. Hank flashed him a grin, and Jay responded with a thumbs-up signal. Then the whistle shrieked, and the puck, in the Eagles' possession, became a black missile flying toward our net. Suddenly

Jay broke through the defense, slithering past the burly Eagle center to snag the puck and shoot it back to Hank.

Hank plunged through an opening, which appeared as if by magic, in the swarm of blue-and-gold jerseys, flying sticks, and flashing skate blades. For an instant he was blocked from my view. Our side went wild, all of us jumping up and down, stamping our feet, and screaming at the top of our lungs. Above the thunder of our enthusiasm, the sharp crack of wood against rubber sounded like a gunshot. The puck went spinning through the air, past the Eagles' flailing goalie, to hit the net. A number flashed on the scoreboard—six to five, our favor. We had won the game.

Linda hugged me. "Wow! Wasn't he fantastic? Did you see the way he plowed right through those stupid Eagles? I don't care if he is shy—he sure knows how to show his stuff out on the ice!"

"He couldn't have done it without Jay's help," I felt obligated to point out for some reason, probably because I was still irritated with Linda for making such a big deal about the possibility of Hank's liking me. But she wasn't paying attention. She went babbling on about the game as we were caught up in the surge of departing fans.

"Hey, Mattie—Linda!" called Sueann Helms, one of the cheerleaders, waving at us as she bobbed past, arm in arm with her Kannonball boyfriend, Curt Thackery, who was walking to the locker room.

I waved back just as she disappeared from view and another familiar figure loomed into sight. Before I could lower my arm, Hank Butterfield, no doubt thinking I was waving at him, cast a shy smile in my direction. His corn-colored hair was curled in damp ringlets around his handsome, flushed face. Whether he was flushed from the thrill of his victory or the embarrassment of having to acknowledge me, I couldn't be sure.

For a long moment, he just stood there as if frozen, looking as if he wanted to say something but didn't have the nerve. Just then, someone who'd been shaking up a bottle of Pepsi released the cap, scattering the crowd with a shower of bubbles. I ducked. When the excitement had died down, Hank had disappeared into the locker room.

Of course, Linda the Sleuth hadn't missed a move. "Didn't I tell you?" she asked, smirking once again.

"I still say you're dreaming," I shot back, annoyed that I was starting to think she might not be so wrong after all. "You can call this one *The Case of the Imaginary Boyfriend.*"

She giggled. "More like *The Mysterious Loves of Mattie Winston.* Remember that guy last year who kept calling you up but never got the nerve to ask you out?"

I groaned. "Brad Devenczeski. How could I forget? But don't you remember? He finally did ask me out—only it was the weekend I was going skiing with my cousin. He must've thought I made it up as an excuse because he never called back after that."

"Doomed to be unlucky in love, I guess," she said, pulling a canary-yellow stocking cap over her short black curls as we met the sub-zero chill of the outdoors.

Linda was only kidding, of course, but she'd hit a sore spot nevertheless. Not that my love life was all that unlucky. I'd had my share of dates, but never with anyone I really felt close to—someone with whom I could share my secret thoughts and those too-crazy-to-talk-about-with-anyone-else dreams. Someone I could really get comfortable with, too, for example the two of us pigging out on pizza and not worrying if the sauce dripped down our chins. A boy who would take me to the prom—and one who would also get up before dawn to dig for clams at the beach with me. Sort of the way it is with Linda and her boyfriend, Glenn Able.

Glenn is a couple of years older than Linda. He goes to Washington State Community College, where they met at a summer writing workshop—he's just as nuts about science fiction as Linda is about mysteries. He's even had one or two of his stories published in sci-fi magazines, which makes him the next best thing to a celestial visitor as far as Linda is concerned.

On the surface they don't seem anything alike. Linda is the short, bouncy-bubbly type. Glenn is tall and serious, with a kind of dreamy, unfocused look. He has a habit of glancing up over your head when he's talking to you, as if he expects to see a falling star or a UFO. But the way they feel about each other is the same. As close as Linda and I are, I've never told her about the twinges of envy I sometimes feel watching her and Glenn together. She'd probably laugh, because it's always the dumbest little things that get to me—like the way they can look at each other and just *know* what the other person is thinking, or the way they automatically fall into step when they're walking together.

If I tried that with Hank, I'd probably trip.

Out in the parking lot we ran into Sueann again, who was waiting for Curt. "Why don't you guys come with us?" she urged. "As soon as Curt gets changed, we're going over to MacDougal's to have pizza to celebrate."

Linda and I looked at each other, and suddenly all thoughts of the cottage cheese-and-grapefruit diet we'd sworn undying allegiance to only that morning flew right out the window.

By the time we got there, MacDougal's was filled with jostling bodies. Music pulsed from the jukebox, and the air was spiced with the tempting aroma of pizza hot from the oven. Rough cedar-planked walls and checkered curtains tied back over steam-frosted windows gave it a homey feeling that wasn't "put-on," as it was at some of the newer places in town.

"Over here, you guys!" yelled someone from a table full of kids we knew. We grabbed chairs, and everyone moved over to make room for us.

As I scooted into my chair, Linda jabbed me in the ribs to get my attention. I looked over—and caught Hank Butterfield's eye once again. He was sitting at the table right next to ours. Both of us looked away quickly. The next time I risked a glance out of the corner of my eye, he was absorbed in conversation with Jay, who was sitting beside him. After that, I caught him sneaking furtive looks in my direction every few minutes.

Suddenly I was aware of how warm it was in there.

"Let's go," I whispered to Linda. "I'm not really all that hungry."

"Are you kidding? I'm starved! All I ate today was that dumb grapefruit and cottage cheese. Man cannot live on grapefruit and cottage cheese alone." Emphasizing her point, she pounced upon a tray that was making the rounds and snatched up a dripping wedge of pizza, half of which she promptly stuffed into her mouth.

Since Linda was driving, I decided not to press it. Instead, I helped myself to a slice of pepperoni, nibbling distractedly and listening to everyone at the table rave about the game.

"Hey, Hank, nice going!" Pete Hansen called.

Hank grinned, then suddenly, to my horror, he was getting up and walking over to our table. Blushing furiously, he leaned toward me, stammering something unintelligible.

"What?" I moved closer so I could hear what he was saying above the din of the jukebox and chatter. Maybe all he wanted was the saltshaker or some extra napkins.

"I was wondering if you, uh, would like to dance?" he repeated.

He looked so helpless all of a sudden—not like the confident dynamo he'd been on the ice less than an hour before—that I couldn't help but feel sorry for him. Besides, he *was* cute. I found myself wondering seriously what it would be like to get to know Hank.

Propelled by Linda's elbow, I rose to my feet. "Sure," I said, returning his smile.

In his relief Hank grabbed for my hand too quickly, knocking over a paper cup of root beer. He stared in horror as it splattered onto my jeans before dribbling down to form a puddle on the floor. Fast-thinking Linda grabbed a wad of napkins and began mopping it up, chattering a mile a minute to cover up for Hank's embarrassment.

"It's OK," I put in quickly, giving him what I hoped was a reassuring look. "Honestly. It's no big deal. I was going to wash these jeans anyhow." Before he could withdraw, I slipped my hand into his.

Hank seemed to loosen up when we got out on the dance floor, but he was still pretty quiet. *The strong, silent type,* I thought. We warmed up with a couple of fast numbers, then a really slow, romantic song came on. Shyly Hank slid his arms around my waist. I could feel the tensed muscles in his chest as I nestled my face against his sweater. I closed my eyes, letting myself imagine, just for a moment, that *he* was the one. . . .

The song ended, and Hank stepped back as if unsure of what to do next. But I could tell from the way he was grinning that he'd enjoyed himself as much as I had. Suddenly I was aware of how blue his eyes were—a neon blue, fringed with golden lashes. Why hadn't I ever noticed them before? I wanted to reach up and coil one of his damp blond curls around my finger.

He cleared his throat. "Do you dance a lot?" he asked. "You're really good."

"I'm not the athletic type, but I do like music," I told him. "I've played the piano since I was seven."

"You must be pretty good."

"OK, I guess. Mostly I play just because I enjoy it. I mean, I don't think I'd ever make a career of it or anything. Except for teaching— right now I'm giving lessons to little kids."

"Really?" He looked genuinely impressed. "That's great."

I was searching around for something else to fill in the gap in our conversation when luckily the music started up again and we were whirled into a sphere of pulsing sound and movement, where words were no longer necessary.

Over Hank's shoulder, I glanced at Linda, who was dancing with Pete. She grinned and gave me a knowing wink, mouthing the words, *I told you so*.

Chapter Two

The first thing that greeted me when I arrived home was the sight of Barbara lying on the living room carpet in her sleek black leotard. To the beat of loud rock music from the stereo, she was swinging her arms and pumping her right leg up and down. She saw me, smiled a hello, then started on the left leg.

"Hi," I said. "Working on a new routine?"

Barbara teaches Jazzercise, which, besides earning her a good salary, keeps her in fantastic shape. She's my stepmother, but most people, when they first meet us, mistake her for my older sister. Actually, I suppose she could be, since she's only thirteen years older than I am. I guess thirteen is an unlucky number for some, but Barbara and I get along fine—now.

There were a few rough spots when she and Dad got married three years ago. I was a rebellious thirteen-year-old, still hurting from my parents' divorce, so naturally I blamed Barbara for the whole thing. She was an easy target. I can remember one really awful fight we had where I told her it was all her fault— that *she* was the reason my mom and dad weren't living together. I started to cry, and I said a lot of other nasty things, but Barb just sat there, taking it calmly and looking more sorry for me than angry.

"All this must seem pretty scary to you," she said at last in a quiet voice. "But you want to know something? I'm scared, too. Do you think it might be a little easier if we tried helping each other out once in a while?"

It was exactly the right thing for her to say. After that, I stopped thinking only about myself and started thinking more about how Dad and my sister, Nita, and Barb must

18

feel. Little by little, I realized I didn't really hate Barb; in fact, I actually liked her.

One of the things I like most about her is that she has never tried to take my mother's place. I see my mom a lot, but I don't live with her. We all decided in the beginning that it would be best for Nita and me to stay with Dad, since Mom's job as a buyer includes a lot of traveling.

The song ended, and Barb collapsed on the rug. "Twelve new routines a month. I don't know how they expect us to do it!" She pushed a handful of frizzy dark hair out of her eyes. "But of course the hardest part is making it all look easy."

"You'll manage."

There are two other Jazzercise instructors in Port Kearney, but Barb's morning class is by far the most popular. Most of the women, I'm sure, find it hard to believe that size-six Barbara, with her impish looks and nonstop energy, is stepmother to two teenagers and mother of a one-year-old as well.

Barb got up to change the record. "How was the game? Did the Kannonballs cream the Eagles?"

I gave her a quick rehash of the game,

concentrating on the highlights, including Hank's final, victorious goal. Barbara is very athletic, so I knew her interest was genuine.

"Sounds exciting," she commented. "I wish I could've been there myself, but I probably would have had more luck finding a needle in a haystack than a babysitter tonight."

I knew she wasn't trying to make me feel bad, but whenever she said things like that, I couldn't help feeling a twinge of guilt. She and Dad would have liked to get out more, but they seldom pressured Nita or me to baby-sit. Zac wasn't an easy baby to take care of—he was cutting several teeth and was pretty cranky about it. But silently I resolved to volunteer my services more often in the future.

"Dad home?" I asked, grabbing an apple from the sideboard near the kitchen. Suddenly I was hungry again.

"He had an emergency call out at the Lucketts'," she told me. "One of their cows, I think. He'll probably be pretty late."

My dad is a veterinarian. Port Kearney is mostly a farming community, so even though he has a small clinic and office downtown, he still has to make a lot of calls to outlying areas.

Barb put on a new record, a Stevie Wonder album. Listening to "Ribbons in the Sky," a song Hank and I had danced to that night, I thought of the way his hand had pressed against the small of my back, moving up and down ever so slightly as we swayed to the music. My skin prickled deliciously at the memory.

It was our last dance. Afterward, Hank had offered to drive me home, but I told him I was with Linda—a decision I regretted, since she had spent the whole way home haranguing me about turning Hank down.

"Just think," she had said, "he might have kissed you."

From the way she was talking, I could tell she was in one of her missing-Glenn moods. At that moment, he was off at a Star Trek convention in Seattle. He was only gone for the week, but judging from how Linda was acting, you'd think it was a year.

"Well," Linda had pressed, "you *do* want him to kiss you, don't you?"

Later, thinking over Linda's question, I had to admit the idea of Hank's kissing me *had* popped into my head. He might be shy, I thought, but kissing was one activity that didn't require much talking. Maybe he was as good at kissing as he was at firing pucks into nets. The image conjured up by that comparison caused me to giggle right out loud.

"What's so funny?" asked Nita, slowly walking into the room with a Webster's Dictionary balanced on top of her head in an effort to improve her posture.

"You," I said, teasing her, unable to resist making fun of her. "You're tall enough already. That book adds three inches to your height. You look like an advertisement for higher education."

She made an attempt at glaring down her nose at me, but her concentration broke, and the dictionary toppled to the floor. "Now see what you made me do!" she wailed.

"Oh, Mattie." Barb laughed. "When I was your age, what I wanted more than anything in the world was to be *tall*. You both should be thankful that you inherited your father's height."

I'm five-seven, which isn't exactly towering, but Barb was right about Nita. She was thirteen, and already five feet nine and a half inches tall. I remember when she came home from school in tears because some stupid kid in her class had called her a baby giraffe. Barb had calmed her down by showing her pictures of the glamorous models in *Vogue*, pointing out that most of them were over five-nine. Since then, Nita has had it in her mind to be the next Cheryl Tiegs. Actually, I suppose she could be a model—but not the kind in *Cosmopolitan*. My little sister would be perfect for an ad to sell milk, for example.

Nita retrieved the book, propping it back on top of her curly chestnut hair. "I'm practicing for the Winter Festival tryouts. You're supposed to be at least fourteen to enter, but they let me sign up since I'll be fourteen by the time they have the contest."

"What contest?" I asked.

Nita sighed, giving me one of her how-can-anyone-be-so-dumb looks. "For the festival queen, of course. I don't really think I'll win, but if I'm lucky I'll get picked as one of the attendants."

Every year during January a bunch of girls swallowed their embarrassment and get

23

up in front of an auditorium full of people to be judged for their talent and beauty. I was glad I wasn't one of them. I've always enjoyed the sled races and snow-sculpture contest that are part of the Winter Festival, but the beauty contest is something I've never been interested in.

"You could try out, too, if you wanted," said Nita, obviously wanting someone beside her to bolster up her own confidence. "You could play the piano. I'll bet the judges would really be impressed."

"What are you going to do for talent?" I asked, to change the subject.

Nita grimaced. "I haven't decided yet. You're talking about someone whose biggest talents are cooking and eating."

"Why don't you bake a cake and devour it up on stage?" I suggested with a straight face.

Nita snatched a small pillow off the couch and hurled it at me. I ducked just in time, and it sailed past me, hitting Barb instead. Laughing, Barb picked it up and threw it back at Nita.

At that moment the phone rang. Nita

dived into the kitchen to answer it, returning with a glum expression. "It's for you, Mattie," she said, adding in disgust, "a boy."

I knew she'd been hoping it was Ken Hollis, a boy her age who'd moved down the street a few weeks before. He was the object of her first serious crush.

I wondered who would be calling me that late. Hank? A bubble of panic floated up from my stomach, lodging in my throat. *Was he going to ask me out?* I found myself hoping it was Hank—and hoping he would ask me out, though only heaven knew what we would find to talk about. . . .

"Hi, Mattie," an oddly husky voice greeted me.

"Hank?"

He chuckled, making a low easy sound. "Yeah, yours truly."

"You sound—I don't know, different somehow."

"That's because I have to keep my voice down if I want any privacy. The phone's in the kitchen."

"Why don't you get another phone?"

"Believe me, I'd like nothing better. The thing is, we can't afford it right now."

"Oh." I was a little embarrassed for having pried into his family's financial situation. I wondered if Hank was embarrassed, too.

He didn't seem to be. "Actually," he said, "the truth is, I'm just hoping to impress you with my sexy whisper."

I couldn't believe it was the same Hank who had been so tongue-tied earlier that night when he walked me across the parking lot to Linda's car. But, I reasoned, a lot of people had trouble warming up at first. Maybe Hank was just a slow starter.

"You sound more like Humphrey Bogart with bronchitis," I said, giggling.

"It was supposed to be Al Pacino with asthma, but you get the prize anyway."

"What prize?"

"A date with me next Saturday night."

"You make it sound so irresistible," I answered sarcastically.

"I can't help it if I'm irresistible, can I?"

I laughed. "Not only irresistible, but conceited, too."

"Does that mean you'll go out with me?"

"How can I resist?"

"Hey." He grew serious. "I want to tell

26

you—you really looked great tonight. I mean, you always look great, but—"

I could feel him beginning to get in over his head, so I quickly changed the subject. "I didn't get a chance to tell you, either, but you were really fantastic at the game. That last goal was something else. Wow! I thought I was going to go deaf with all the yelling. Do you think the Kannonballs will win the championship this year?"

"I'm counting on it. I just hope Jamie's ankle heals before next week. We're playing these guys from Oak Harbor, and I hear this year's team is pretty tough. We'll need all the help we can get."

"It's nothing serious with Jamie, is it?"

"Just a mild sprain, but you know how those things are if you don't take care of them."

"I broke my ankle once when I went skiing," I told him. "The stupid part was I hadn't even made it out to the slopes when it happened. I tripped going down the stairs of the lodge."

Again, that throaty laugh. "I'll bet you never lived that one down."

"I wanted everyone to think I'd had an accident while I was racing downhill or something exciting like that, but my sister kept opening her big mouth and telling people the truth, that I tripped on my own boots."

"Yeah, I know how sisters can be."

"How many do you have?"

"Well, uh, none actually. But I hang around Jay a lot, and he's got three. They really know how to give him a hard time."

"One's enough for me, thanks. Right now Nita's going crazy trying to figure out what she can do for the talent part of the Miss Winter Festival contest."

"You mean talent doesn't run in your family?"

"Don't ask me how I got started playing the piano," I said. "Dad's got a tin ear, and Mom always claimed she couldn't sit still long enough to learn an instrument."

"I know what you mean. Neither of my parents is very athletic. I really don't know how I got so interested in hockey. But in case you're thinking I'm just a dumb jock, I like music, too."

"Classical?"

"Well, yeah—some. But I was thinking more of that new group that's going to be playing in town this weekend."

"The Class Act? Oh, I just love them!"

"Good." He sounded pleased with himself. "Because that's where we're going Saturday night."

"Really? That's great."

"I was hoping it might help make up for me spilling Coke all over you tonight."

"Root beer."

"Huh?"

"It was root beer, but who cares? You can spill it on me anytime if this is how I get repaid."

We both laughed. There was a pause, then Hank said, "Well, I guess I'd better go. It's really been fun talking to you, though."

"Yeah, I've enjoyed it, too," I answered, surprised to discover I really meant it.

Funny, I thought, how you can judge a person to be one way and he turns out to be completely different. Hank had seemed so quiet and shy, and yet on the phone I'd discovered that he had a sense of humor and a way of looking at things that made me suspect we had a lot in common.

First impressions *were* deceiving.

"Well—see ya," came Hank's husky good-bye.

"Bye."

I hung up feeling warm all over.

Chapter Three

The next morning I caught up with Linda before first period and told her about Hank's asking me out. I'd been dying to talk to her since the night before, but by the time Hank and I hung up, I knew it would be too late.

"I couldn't believe it," I told her. "He was so much fun to talk to. Not at all shy like he was at MacDougal's. Boy, was I wrong about him!"

"Just as I suspected," Linda said, giving me one of her mysterious smiles.

"What do you mean?"

"Well—we've seen him in glorious action

31

out on the ice. Nothing shy about *that*. That's the real Hank. I suspected all he really needed was just a little encouragement to bring him out of his shell."

"Leave it to Nancy Drew."

"Don't laugh. There was a case in the last Roberta Reese mystery I read, *The Masquerade Murders.* You see, there was this man who could only be himself with his true love when he was wearing a mask."

"Ugh. It doesn't sound very romantic."

"The point is, maybe Hank felt more comfortable talking to you over the phone because you couldn't see him. He was invisible, so to speak."

I sighed in exasperation. "Linda, you have the answer for everything, don't you?"

"Well, it makes sense doesn't it?"

"In a funny sort of a way—yeah, I guess so."

We were late for psych, but fortunately Mrs. Grodin was doing one of her slide-lectures, and the room was dark enough for us to slide unnoticed into our seats. A diagram of the human brain flashed onto the screen.

"How gross," muttered Gayle Shorter beside me before going back to polishing her nails. I wondered what they would look like when the lights came on again.

Mrs. Grodin was using her pointer to indicate which areas of the brain control which functions. She must've gotten pretty carried away, because suddenly the pointer jabbed right through the screen, dissecting the brain neatly in two. I'm sure it wasn't really her fault, since the screen—like every other piece of equipment at Port Kearney—was about five thousand years old, but everyone started cracking up and giving her a hard time about it anyway.

"That's what you call a split personality," shouted Kurt Dorfmeyer from the back of the room.

"Does anyone know what a split personality *is*?" Mrs. Grodin asked in a faltering attempt to regain control of the class.

"Yeah," someone said. "I saw a movie about it on the late show the other night—*Dr. Jekyll and Mr. Hyde*."

"There's no such thing in *real* life," scoffed Carol Bruce, a blond cheerleader who spent most of her time in class reading the magazines she carried around in her binder—stuff like *Seventeen* and *Rolling Stone*. She knew everything there was to know about the true loves of Matt Dillon.

"Actually," Mrs. Grodin said, "there are real-life examples of split personality, although they're very rare, of course. In extreme cases, the person takes on one or more totally separate identities—even down to their names and the way they talk. One man I read about had a personality who spoke fluent Hungarian, but the others didn't understand a word of it."

"Creepy," remarked Melvin St. Clair, draping one lanky leg over the empty seat in front of him. "My dad must be a split personality because my mom's always saying he's like a different person in the morning before he's had his coffee."

Outspoken Suzanne Harte didn't miss her cue to put in, "Sounds like my boyfriend. A perfectly normal person until I'm alone with him at the drive-in. Then he turns into Wolfman."

A fresh outbreak of snickers greeted her remark. But the hilarity died down quickly as Mrs. Grodin, having successfully repaired the screen with a roll of masking tape, resumed the slide show.

In the darkness, Linda passed me a carefully folded square of paper. She'd written, "Maybe H. is a split personality?????"

I crumpled the note in disgust. Honestly, Linda could get *too* carried away sometimes. What would she come up with next? Would she accuse Hank of drinking secret potions and becoming the Mr. Hyde of Port Kearney High? I suppressed a giggle at the thought. Tearing off a piece of paper, I wrote, "Maybe Glenn is an extra-terrestrial???" I passed it back to Linda and was rewarded by a loud snicker of contempt.

"Really, Linda," Mrs. Grodin chided. "I don't see the humor in brain tumors."

By the end of lunchtime, though, I wasn't so sure Linda had been wrong about Hank having a split personality. I'd spotted him in the cafeteria with Jay and had gone over to his table to say hello. Hank smiled as if he were glad to see me, but I couldn't help noticing that he looked uncomfortable. Jay didn't even bother to smile; his expression was a definite scowl. Had I interrupted something?

"Hi, Mattie," Hank said. "You—you want to sit down?"

"That's OK," I said, getting the definite feeling from Jay that I'd broken in on something. "I can see you're busy."

"Naw," muttered Jay with a dark look, cramming in the last of his hamburger. "I was just leaving anyway. See you later."

Reluctantly I slid into Jay's empty place, feeling as if I'd driven him off somehow. Hank wasn't much help, either. He just sat there, looking at me with that funny embarrassed expression, as if we'd reverted to being total strangers once again. Finally, out of nervousness, we both laughed, and immediately the tension was broken.

"What did you think of that quiz Mr. Ricci gave us yesterday?" I asked him.

He rolled his eyes. "I'll be lucky if I got two out of ten right. Jeez, who can remember all that stuff?" He grinned, jabbing his fork into the remains of his sloppy joe.

"I don't think Mr. Ricci will hold it against you. I saw him sneaking into the game last night. I think he's a closet hockey fan."

"Mr. Ricci?" Hank looked up at me, his blue eyes wide with incredulity.

Our government teacher is the most un-athletic-looking person imaginable. He weighs about ninety pounds, is bald except for a few wisps of hair combed over the top of his head, and he wears glasses that look as if they were made from the bottoms of Coke bottles. He's always telling us we should think less about our bodies and more about our minds.

"It was just a joke," I explained.

Hank laughed. "Yeah—I thought so." He lowered his voice. "I got the tickets."

"Tickets?"

"The concert—remember?" He was stricken suddenly by that same panicky expression he'd had when he spilled the root beer. "You still want to go, don't you?"

"Oh, that—of course I do."

He blushed with relief, and I thought again how handsome he was. "OK if I pick you up at eight, then?"

"Sure, that's fine," I said.

"Well—" He rose hastily as if he wanted to leave before I changed my mind. "I guess I should get going. You know how it is."

I watched him for a minute before he disappeared into the crowd. I noticed the easy swing of his muscular shoulders, the way his rumpled blond hair curled over the back of his collar. He was everything a girl could want in a boyfriend, I thought.

Then why was I feeling that way? Almost as if I were—disappointed.

Hank had been friendly enough, and it was clear he wanted to go out with me. But we were back to square one as far as conversation went. Talking to him on the phone had been so easy—why did he have to get so uncomfortable when we were together?

I thought about that stuff Linda had said about masks. Obviously the phone was Hank's mask.

Unless Hank's problem was more complicated, like a split personality.

The idea was so ridiculous, I wanted to laugh. I'd been hanging around with Linda so long I was even starting to think like her.

We were walking home from school when it started to snow. Feathery flakes swirled down from a slate-colored sky, dusting the sidewalk and whitewashing the dirty remains of the last snow. Linda closed her eyes and threw her head back; she liked the feel of the snow melting against her face, she said.

"It's a little like getting kissed, don't you think?" she asked, shaking the powder from her curls and giving an exuberant laugh.

"Glenn must be a cold kisser," I said teasingly.

"Not half so cold as you're going to be when I get through with you!" She advanced on me, eyes glittering as she brandished a hastily formed snowball.

I ducked just in time, but as soon as I turned around to scoop up a handful of snow, one of Linda's missiles whacked me between the shoulder blades. I repaid her with a double-barreled whammy: one snowball caught her on the ear, the other just above the knee. Linda scooted behind a lamppost, collapsing against it in helpless giggles when she realized what little protection it was.

"It'll probably be the year 2000 before Hank gets around to kissing *me* at the rate we're going," I gasped when I'd gotten my breath back.

"Glenn was like that at first," Linda confessed.

"You mean shy?"

"Not exactly. He's just got his head in the clouds most of the time."

"What did you do about it?"

Her cheeks were pink with cold, but they grew even pinker. Linda and I were close, but some things are too private to talk about, even with your best friend. This was the first time we had discussed the *intimate* details of her romance with Glenn.

"Well," she admitted sheepishly, "if you want to know the truth: I tricked him into kissing me."

"You didn't!"

She nodded. "It was our third date, and I didn't think he was *ever* going to get around to it. Sooo—I told him I was on this part in the book I was writing where the hero gives mouth-to-mouth resuscitation to this drowning woman he's just saved. I asked him if I could practice on him just to get the hang of it."

I gaped at her in astonishment. "And he believed you?"

"Who cares?" She laughed. "Anyway, once we got started I could tell it was what he'd wanted to do all along—only he just didn't have the nerve to try it."

"I'm not sure it makes sense," I said, "but I think I know what you mean."

She looked at me. "The point is, you can't always wait for the boy to make the first move. And I don't mean that you should attack him, either. Things like this sometimes take delicate maneuvering."

"Mouth-to-mouth resuscitation is out, definitely out," I informed her flatly.

"You're right. It was a pretty dumb idea, but I was desperate."

"Well, I'm not all that desperate about Hank. In fact, I'm not sure yet how I feel about him."

We took turns brushing the snow off each other before continuing on.

"It doesn't always strike you like lightning," Linda agreed. "I know. With Glenn it just sort of sneaked up on me."

I looked down at my boots, kicking up little flurries of powder as I walked. "I like Hank, but—"

"But what?"

"Well, I just wish I could figure him out.

41

One minute he's one way, and the next minute he's another. It's crazy, but I'm almost starting to believe your theory about a split personality."

"Never mind about that," she said. "I was only kidding."

"What is it, then?"

"For one thing, you hardly know each other. For another, the school cafeteria is hardly the place for romance."

She was right, I thought. I was worrying about nothing—as usual. Hank would be fine once we were alone on a date. I tried to picture us together, Hank's arms around me, tightening as he moved his face closer to mine. . . .

For some reason, the image wouldn't stick. I kept hearing in my mind Hank's low easy laugh over the phone, remembering the way it had warmed me. What I really wanted was for Hank to make me feel that way again. Special. I had felt it the night before, the two of us reaching out, stretching toward some sort of closeness—then abruptly, we'd snapped apart again.

"Love!" I groaned out loud, rattling the

42

branches of a sycamore tree and showering us with a fresh coating of snow. "It's more complicated than a Rubik's Cube."

"Yeah," Linda said, sighing, "but think of all the fun you can have while you're figuring it out."

Chapter Four

Barbara was in the midst of trying to teach Nita a jazz routine when I got home. Unfortunately, Nita is not so coordinated as Barb. As I walked in, Nita's arm flew out and knocked over one of the table lamps. Zac, who was across the room, tottering on unsteady legs, let out a screech and plopped down on his backside. I scooped him up, bribing him into silence with a mushy-looking zwieback I'd retrieved from his high chair.

Nita wasn't so easily consoled. "It's no use," she said, moaning. "Let's face it—I'm just not cut out to be a dancer."

44

"It's not something you become overnight," I told her. "Maybe if you practiced some more—"

"Easy for you to say—you've got a talent. You're not a total washout." She flopped down on the couch in an untidy sprawl.

"Thanks for the compliment," I replied frostily. "But for your information, I didn't just sit down at the piano one day and start playing Mozart. I had to work my way up from 'Mary Had a Little Lamb' and 'Twinkle, Twinkle, Little Star' first."

"Yeah, I remember," she said, giggling and clapping her hands over her ears for emphasis.

I decided I would ignore that one. Nita can be very immature at times.

"Mattie's right," put in Barb. "It takes a lot of practice to be good at *anything*."

Fresh despair overtook Nita as she wailed, "But I've only got three more weeks. What am I going to do?"

"We'll think of something," I told her, but it didn't sound too hopeful.

As it turned out, it was Mom who came up with the answer to Nita's dilemma. She's head buyer for a chain of clothing stores, and she'd stopped by unexpectedly before one of her out-of-town buying trips. Of course, Barb invited her to stay for dinner.

I was surprised when Mom accepted. Despite the fact that my parents remained friendly after the divorce, it's uncomfortable when Dad, Mom, and Barb are together. Mom and Barb are always bending over backward to be polite. *Too* polite, in my opinion. It's obvious that Barb feels somewhat swept to one side by the tendency Mom has to take over any situation she's in. I know, because sometimes I feel that way around her, too. Mom is just so—sure of herself. It's scary. Dad used to say she could do anything she put her mind to.

After dinner I watched Mom as she adjusted the pins on a dress Nita was making. I often think Mom could have been a model herself. She's tall and slender, with wide-set grayish-blue eyes and blond hair that fluffs softly around her face, making her look younger than she really is. Ever since I can remember, people have been telling me what a pretty mother I have. I know what they're really saying is that it's too bad neither Nita nor I look anything like her.

"There," she pronounced, standing back and smiling as she admired Nita's handiwork. "A perfect fit. You did a nice job. And you're lucky you're tall enough to show it off, honey."

"Too bad being tall isn't a talent," I teased, explaining to Mom about the talent competition Nita was entered in.

"Maybe it is," Mom said, eyeing Nita with a thoughtful expression. "You have style—and you know how to sew. Why couldn't you model a dress you designed yourself?"

Nita's response was to throw her arms around Mom in a grateful hug. "Mom, you're fantastic! It's a great idea. Why didn't I think of it?"

I could see that Barb, stacking alphabet blocks with Zac over in the corner, was trying hard not to listen—and even harder not to look as if she felt left out.

"I'll only be in San Francisco for a few days," Mom said. "When I get back, we'll go shopping for material. Mattie, you come, too. We'll make a day of it—drive into Seattle and have lunch at the Sheraton. What do you say?"

"Great," I said, not wanting to sound *too* excited for Barb's sake.

Nita, however, was in ecstasy. She glided up and down in front of the fireplace, twirling around every few steps as she practiced the way a model walks down a runway. She was doing pretty well until she stepped on one of Zac's rubber toys which emitted a loud squeak and caused her to stumble. We all burst into laughter, even Nita.

Dad, who hadn't said a word the whole time, finally chimed in, "You should use it in your act. A little humor never hurts."

"Oh, Dad!" Nita rolled her eyes in disgust. "This is serious."

He smiled, lifting his shaggy brows over the tops of his reading glasses. "When you're thirteen, everything is serious business."

"I remember—" Barb started to say.

"Speaking of business," Mom interrupted with a glance at her wristwatch, "I have a plane to catch. Mattie, honey," she said, looking at me, "how would you like to drive me to the airport? Then you can use my car while I'm gone."

I stood there for a minute, not knowing what to say. I'd promised Dad and Barb I would baby-sit for Zac so they could go to a movie, and the airport was in Seattle, a good hour's drive from where we lived. Sensing my indecision, Barb quickly stepped in to rescue the situation.

"You girls go along with your mother," she piped in brightly—a little too brightly. "Your dad and I can go to the movies another night."

Not to be outdone in politeness, Mom offered just as quickly to take Zac along with us, but Barb said it was his bedtime and practically pushed us out the door. As usual, Dad stayed out of it, choosing to bury his head in the latest copy of *The Journal of Veterinary Medicine* rather than step into the middle of a battle of politeness between two women.

Graciously Mom shook Barb's hand. "Thank you, Barbara, dear. It was a *lovely* dinner. It's not often I get to enjoy a home-cooked meal these days."

She was being sincere, but Barb blushed with embarrassment, knowing the meal wasn't one of her better ones. She'd been so busy feeding Zac, she'd forgotten about the tuna casserole, and it had gotten a little burned around the edges.

"You're welcome anytime, Alice," she said.

At that moment, I wanted to hug them both, but instead I ducked outside, feeling like a coward who was being torn in two directions.

"I know what you mean," Hank spoke softly into the phone. "It's hard when you love two people, and you feel like you have to choose between them."

Hank had called when I got back from the airport, and we'd been gabbing away for nearly an hour. *It's so easy to confide in him*, I thought. *Underneath it all, we're really two of a kind.*

"I love them in different ways," I said. "Barb could never take my mother's place. She's more like a big sister. Special—in her own way. She really tries hard, too."

"Have you ever told her how you feel?"

"No. We don't talk about things like that. You know those comic strips you see where there's this question mark hanging over someone's head? Well, that's how it is with Barb and me."

"Only life isn't a comic strip, right?"

I laughed. "Sometimes I wish it were."

"I can just see it. 'Mattie, Girl Marvel, Fights an Attack of the Grungy Guilts!' "

"Why do I feel so guilty?"

"Because you're trying to make everyone happy at once. And that's impossible. I remember once when I was a real little kid and both my grandmas wanted to take me shopping on my birthday. Nana was the one I liked best, but she always bought me boring things like books and pajamas. I knew Grandma Cassidy would get me what I really wanted—a remote-control model airplane."

"What did you do?"

"I worried about it so much, I got a stomachache and had to stay home. Which was really dumb, because in the end I got it all anyway: the books and pajamas *and* the model airplane."

"I'm not sure that story has a moral," I pointed out.

"Sure it does. All that worrying made me miss out on my birthday cake, didn't it?"

"So if I quit worrying about Mom and Barb, I'll get to eat birthday cake?"

"Don't forget the vanilla ice cream."

"OK." I laughed. "But you'd better make it rocky road. I hate vanilla."

"You do? So do I. I guess that's what makes us so compatible."

We both laughed.

"You're crazy," I said, "but smart. How did you get to be so smart?"

"Smart! Obviously, you didn't see my last report card."

"That bad, huh?"

"It could've been worse, I guess. But it's hard finding the time to study with all the practicing I have to do. It gets to be a drag when you never have time for anything else."

"Do you like to dig for clams?" I asked impulsively.

"I don't know—I've never tried it."

"You'd have to get up early—while it's still dark. There's this cove I know of, but you have to hike a little way to get to it."

There was a pause, then Hank said in a strangely flat voice, "Sounds like fun."

"It was just an idea," I said. "We don't have to if you don't want to."

"No—I really would like to sometime." There was another, longer pause before he added, "You're really full of surprises, you know that, Mattie? What else do you like besides rocky road ice cream and digging for clams?"

"I like talking to you," I blurted out, surprised at my own boldness.

"Likewise." His voice sounded even huskier than usual. "The question is—what do we do for an encore?"

"I don't know." I giggled, blushing. I was glad he couldn't see me.

Just then my father poked his head through the doorway into my room, where I lay curled on my bed with the extension glued to my ear. He frowned, pantomiming that it was time for me to hang up.

"I gotta go," I told Hank.

"I know," he whispered. "Me, too."

"Bye."

"Bye." I hung up the phone.

Dad was gazing at me with a knowing look. My father is a man of few words, but a master of knowing looks. He says he gets it from being around animals all day long.

"Must be somebody special," he commented in an offhand way that didn't hide the curiosity in his light blue eyes. "I can't remember the last time I had to pry you away from the phone. Now, with Nita it's another matter. . . ."

My sister's attachment to the telephone

is legendary in our house. We have a family joke that she and her best friend, Katie, are really Siamese twins—joined at the ear.

"I don't know," I hedged, finally admitting, "I hope so."

Was that the way Dad had felt about Barb in the beginning? I knew he'd loved Mom, too, because he'd told me so, but we had never really talked about his feelings for Barb. Maybe he was afraid I wouldn't understand how he could love two people in different ways at different times. Probably he didn't think I was ready for love.

He was probably right—until Hank. I wondered if maybe, just maybe, I was falling in love with Hank.

Dad stood in the doorway for another minute, a tall figure framed by the light from the hallway. He looked as if he wanted to say something more, but instead he only came quietly into the room and kissed me lightly on the top of my head, saying, "Good night. Sleep tight, and don't let the kangaroos bite."

That was his standard line at bedtime when I was a little girl, but he hadn't used it in years. It started when they named me Matilda, after the Australian song "Waltzing

Matilda." No one ever called me anything but Mattie, but Dad still teased me about kangaroos once in a while. He even gave me a stuffed kangaroo last Christmas. I was surprised he had remembered—it had been so long ago.

I kissed him back, liking the scratchiness of his chin against my skin. "G'night, Dad."

I didn't want to think about kangaroos that night. I wanted to curl up thinking only about Hank—and try to sort out all the emotions that went with my thoughts.

Chapter Five

"Gee, Mattie, you look great."

I was glad Hank approved of the outfit I'd chosen for the concert: my best pair of jeans, a shell-pink sweater and my maroon cowboy boots. He was dressed casually, too, in jeans and a pullover.

I was happy to notice that Nita was definitely in awe of my date for the evening. Tall, blond, handsome Hank—who wouldn't be jealous?

"Do you want a Coke or something?" she offered, obviously hoping to prolong his stay. "I think there's some fried chicken left over from dinner."

"Uh, no thanks." Hank cast a quick glance in my direction. "We should probably get going."

My father shook Hank's hand. They were about the same height, but Hank probably outweighed him by about twenty-five pounds.

"It was nice meeting you, Hank," he said. Winking, he added, "Take care you don't blast your eardrums apart. I've heard how noisy these rock concerts can get."

"Better than being put to sleep by Lawrence Welk," I quipped, earning a laugh from Barb. Dad was always giving her a hard time about her Jazzercise tapes being too loud.

Barbara hugged me. "You have a good time, you hear? And don't worry about your eardrums. If Zac hasn't shattered them by now, they'll hold up through anything."

Hank was silent until we got out to his car, a blue Toyota hatchback that barely contained his six-foot-four frame.

"Sorry I couldn't stick around and talk to you at lunch today. Jay and I had a meeting with the coach." He squeezed my hand. "You're not mad, are you?"

"No," I said. I wasn't—not anymore. Mystified was more like it. At school, whenever I

57

ran into Hank with Jay, I got the definite feeling I wasn't wanted. Did Jay think I was trying to monopolize all of Hank's time? I remembered how I'd felt when Linda started dating Glenn. Until then, we'd always done everything together; she was always there. I could call her up on a Saturday afternoon and ask her if she wanted to see a movie with me that night. But once she started seeing Glenn, if I wanted to go to a movie with her on a Saturday night, I had to call a week in advance to make sure she and Glenn hadn't planned something. It was an awful thing to admit, but I had resented Glenn at first. I suppose it was only natural, and I had gotten over it. Was that the way Jay felt about me?

Casually I remarked, "You and Jay are pretty good friends, aren't you?"

Hank looked at me. "Why the sudden curiosity about Jay?" he asked. It occurred to me then that *he* might be jealous.

"No reason," I said. "I just wondered. You two hang around together a lot."

"Yeah—Jay's a good man. In fact, if it wasn't for him, you wouldn't be going to the concert tonight."

"Why is that?"

58

"I couldn't get another ticket—they were all sold out. Jay and I got ours a couple of weeks ago, so I talked him into selling me his so I could take you instead."

No wonder Jay resented me! If it had been me left out in the cold, I would have been furious. It was an unwritten code that members of the opposite sex took precedence over friends, but I'd always thought that was pretty unfair. Good friends, in their own way, were just as important as romance.

But instead of speaking out, I only murmured, "That was nice of him."

"Like I said, Jay's a nice guy." Hank grinned. "Besides, I don't think he'll mind the sacrifice so much. He told me he's taking out Janine Hawes tonight."

Somehow I couldn't imagine Janine as Jay's type, but then who was I to say? I didn't even know Jay.

The civic auditorium, where the concert was being held, was packed by the time we arrived. I spotted Glenn and Linda among the crush in the lobby and hurried over to greet them.

"We almost didn't make it." Linda was

laughing breathlessly. "Glenn forgot the tickets, and we had to rush back to get them."

Glenn produced the ticket stubs with a flourish. "Here, Lin, I think you ought to keep these as a souvenir. After all, if it hadn't been for your clever deductions, we never would have found them."

"*He* forgot which jacket he'd left them in," she said, smirking, but it was obvious from the adoring way she clung to him that she didn't hold his absentmindedness against him.

"Leave it to good old Nancy Drew," I couldn't resist putting in. "She does have this incredible knack for figuring things out."

Linda grimaced. "I just hope we can find our seats without being stampeded. Have you ever seen so many people in one place in your life?"

With luck, Hank and I managed to find our seats before the warm-up band came on. He slid his arm around my shoulders as we settled into our seats, his hand a warm pressure against my arm. I turned to smile at him. Suddenly I was very glad to be there, in spite of my earlier doubts about Hank. I could tell he didn't feel as awkward around me.

Our phone conversations were mostly responsible for that. I was getting to know a side of Hank that I don't think he showed to many people.

The warm-up band was more noise than music, but the Class Act, the main attraction, more than made up for it. By the end of their first set, they had us singing the words along with them and stamping our feet. They finished up with a long, smooth version of their latest hit, "I Didn't Love You Until I Lost You."

Abruptly Hank and I were caught up in the madhouse crush of everybody trying to push out the exits at once. A group of boys jostled us, and Hank tightened his arm around me protectively, steering me clear of them.

"So—what did you think?" he asked when we were finally outside and could hear ourselves above the din.

"Fantastic! They were really terrific."

"I'm glad you liked it."

"Didn't you?"

"Oh, sure—I like music." He paused under a streetlight, the soft glow turning his tousled blond curls a burnished gold. Our breath punctuated the chill air with puffs of vapor. "I guess it's just sitting still that gets to me."

"I know what you mean," I said, lying. I love being active, but I also love the times when I can sit back and listen to good music or enjoy a good book.

"Are you hungry?" Hank asked when we'd gotten back to the car. "Boy, I sure am!"

What I really wanted was to go somewhere private and quiet where we could talk—really talk.

Before I could answer, Hank asked, "How about MacDougal's?"

My heart sank. At MacDougal's we'd be crammed in with fifty million other people. We'd be lucky if we could hear ourselves think. But since it was obvious Hank didn't share my mood, I kept my disappointment to myself. I didn't want to take the chance of spoiling the good time we were having.

I smiled at him. "What are we waiting for?"

"Mattie, Hank—over here!" I glimpsed a swirl of blond hair, which a moment later materialized as Janine. She waved us over to the booth where she and Jay were sitting.

I wasn't exactly crazy about the idea of sitting with them, but it would have been rude to refuse. I glanced at Jay in apprehension, but as far as he was concerned, I might have been invisible.

"How was the concert?" asked Janine. "We heard it was really super."

"Yeah," Hank said, darting a look at Jay. "It was pretty good."

I wanted to thank Jay for giving me his ticket, even if it wasn't his idea. Maybe I would have gotten up the courage if he hadn't turned to Janine just then and asked, "You want to dance?"

Janine leaped up. "Sure, why not?"

I stood up to let them by, and in doing so, Jay's arm accidentally brushed against mine. He drew away as if he'd touched fire. Startled by his reaction, I froze and stood staring into his beautiful brown eyes. His own gaze quickly dropped, and he mumbled an apology.

I watched the two of them link arms as they melted into the crowd on the dance floor.

"Do you feel like dancing?" Hank asked me, his large square fingers curling over my hand.

"Not really," I said. "Would—would you mind very much if we didn't stay? We could get something to eat at my house." I couldn't explain to Hank how uncomfortable I felt being around Jay. He wouldn't understand.

Hank shrugged. "Sure—no problem."

An hour later, we sat at the antique oak table in our kitchen, drinking hot cocoa and nibbling on freshly baked ginger brownies.

"These are good," commented Hank. "I don't think I've ever eaten a ginger brownie before."

"We're lucky my sister is spending the night with her friend, or there wouldn't be any left by now."

"Did you make them?"

"Are you kidding?" I laughed.

"Why is it so funny?"

"Well, when it comes to cooking, I'm afraid I have a black thumb—it seems like everything I touch ends up getting burned."

"That's too bad." He looked vaguely disappointed, and I wondered if Hank was expecting me to be the homemaker type, like Lisa Halladay, who brought homemade chocolate chip cookies to school practically every day for her boyfriend. Ugh! I couldn't imagine doing such a thing.

We played a game of checkers, then Hank announced that he had to leave. There was a hockey game the next day, and the coach was strict about curfew, he told me. He held my hand as we walked out to his car, putting his arm around me when he saw that I was shivering. I hadn't bothered to put on my jacket, but I realized it didn't matter as Hank drew me into the warm circle of his embrace.

"Mmmm," Hank murmured against my ear.

We were standing on the curb, our bodies casting a single long shadow along the snowy pavement. His lips brushed gently against mine in a kiss that sent the pool of warmth in my stomach rippling outward. I reached up and coiled a lock of his hair around my finger. It was soft and springy. He smelled of ginger and cold air.

"Good night, Hank," I said when we finally drew apart. "I had a good time tonight."

He grinned. "Me, too. I'll call you. Good night, Mattie." He kissed me once more, then was gone.

Chapter Six

"No, that's G. You want B-flat." I corrected my nine-year-old pupil, guiding her stubby fingers over the piano keys. "There, that's it."

Lucy completed the piece, a simplified version of "The Minute Waltz," with no more mistakes. She beamed up at me, her thin freckled face alight with pride. It was at times like that that I found teaching to be very rewarding.

"You're really making progress, Lucy. Just think—only a few months ago you were playing 'Farmer in the Dell,' and now you're all the way up to Chopin!"

"It's fun," she said shyly. "I mean, the way you teach, it is."

Lucy's older sister Jeanette, a girl in my junior class, arrived home just as I was leaving.

"Hi, Mattie," Jeanette called, skipping up the front steps of their rambling Victorian house. She was a short, plump girl with sparkling blue eyes and a quick, sometimes sarcastic wit. "Teaching the kid more ways to torture our ears, huh?"

Lucy, hovering inside the doorway, responded hotly, "You're just jealous 'cause you can't play!"

"Are you kidding? You mean you missed my concert at Carnegie Hall last week?" She managed to tweak one of her sister's braids before Lucy retreated squawking into the house.

Jeanette turned her attention to me. "How's 'Hunk' Butterfield these days? Boy, speaking of jealous, I'd give anything to trade places with you."

I blushed, shifting the stack of music books under my arm. "He's OK, I guess."

Her eyebrows shot up. "You guess? You mean you're not madly in love with him yet?"

"We've only gone out a couple of times!" I

protested laughingly. A grand total of two dates—including the movie he'd taken me to—did not exactly make us a hot item.

"Is he taking you to the Winter Festival dance?" she pressed. Jeanette and I had never been close friends, and I wondered why she was suddenly so curious about my plans.

"He hasn't asked me yet." I realized once I'd said it that the "yet" was a telltale sign that I was expecting him to.

"He will." She gave me a meaningful look designed to imply that she knew more than she was telling.

Her ploy had the desired effect. "How do you know?" I demanded.

"Simple. I overheard him talking to Jay about it in study hall today."

For a moment I had trouble unsticking my voice from my throat. "What did they say?"

"I couldn't hear very much—they were a few tables away, and they were sort of whispering. They were having some kind of argument, I think. Probably something dumb like whether or not he should ask you now or maybe wait a few days."

Hank and Jay were arguing about me!

Chances were Jay was trying to convince him *not* to ask me to the dance at all.

I struggled to hide my emotions from Jeanette. If she knew that Jay Thompson hated me, she'd probably go blabbing it all over school.

"I've gotta go," I muttered, jamming my hands into a pair of navy mittens as I hurried down the steps. "I have another lesson at four-thirty."

All the way through the lesson, I thought about Hank. I managed to speak intelligently about chords and crescendos, but my mind was a million miles away. I knew what Linda would call it: *The Mystery of Hank Butterfield.*

Was I in love with Hank? Was Hank in love with me? Those questions and more whirled inside my head. If anything, the more I got to know Hank, the less sure I was about him.

Linda and I discussed it later, when I stopped by her house on my way home.

"Clue number one," she stated. "He wouldn't ask you out if he didn't want to be with you. And he's always calling you up. Every night this week—that's more than Glenn phones me. Doesn't that tell you anything?"

"Yes." I giggled. "He likes to talk on the telephone."

I sat cross-legged on her bed, facing a huge poster of Sherlock Holmes, which Linda had bought at the school book fair the last fall. Linda was busy painting her toenails an odd purplish-red color. She glanced up at me in disgust, brush poised in midair.

"*I'm* trying to help you get to the bottom of all this, and *you're* talking about phone fetishes," she scolded. "It would serve you right if Hank didn't ask you to the dance after all."

"Oh, Linda." I sighed. "I do like Hank. Maybe I even love him. It's just so complicated. He can be so open sometimes, especially when we're talking on the phone. But other times, I feel like we might as well be strangers."

"Love *is* complicated," she agreed. "Even with Glenn and me."

"But I thought you two got along almost perfectly."

"We do get along well, but Glenn doesn't let me know what he's thinking or feeling as much as I'd like him to. Guys are just that way, I suppose. At least that's what my mother is always saying—that getting my dad to tell her what's on his mind is like pulling teeth."

"At least Glenn is consistent," I pointed out.

"About as consistent as tapioca pudding," she added, giggling while dabbing at a drop of polish with a tissue.

I laughed. "Is that good or bad?"

"Well—" She capped the bottle of polish, then sprawled onto her back and sighed. "Sometimes I wish I could crawl inside his head and know exactly what he was thinking. Then other times, I think, 'Don't be dumb, Linda. If you had him all figured out, you'd be bored stiff!' I guess it's a little like skipping ahead to the end of a book. Once you know how it turns out, you don't want to read it any more."

"I just wish I knew how this story was going to turn out," I said.

"One thing is for sure." Linda stuck her feet in the air, wiggling her toes to make them dry faster. "Chapter two should be *very* interesting."

*   *   *

71

"You sound a little down," Hank observed as we were talking on the phone later that night. "Is something the matter?"

"Nothing much," I hedged.

" 'Nothing much' means it's something," he pressed. "Is it your mom? Have you talked to her lately?"

"She got back from her trip yesterday," I told him, glad to get away from the real reason why I was depressed. "We're going shopping for Nita's dress material this Saturday. Oh, and get this, the two of them roped me into promising I would play ·thė piano for Nita's fashion number. I couldn't get out of it!"

"Sounds like it'll be a good chance for you to show off your own talents," he said, chuckling. Then he added, "You can bet I'll be out there rooting for you."

"I think you'd better save your rooting for Nita," I said. "Just pray she doesn't trip or something. She's a bundle of nerves."

Another reason my sister was so nervous was that her big dream had finally come true— Ken Hollis had asked her to the dance. Now whenever she bumped into him, she was too self-conscious even to talk to him. Heaven only knew how they would act around each other at the dance!

But at least the incident had given me some insight into Hank's occasional attacks of shyness.

"I know," he said. "It's the same thing with me before a game. I get so nervous, my butterflies get a royal workout."

"But you always look so confident!"

"Just an act, but don't tell anyone I said so."

"Were you nervous about asking me out that first time?" I blurted out. I hadn't meant to ask him that, but the words just popped out.

Caught off-guard, Hank became flustered. "Uh, yeah, I guess I kinda was—I wasn't sure what you thought of me."

"I wasn't sure what you thought of me, either."

"Really? Gee, I figured you already knew. I mean, a guy doesn't ask a girl out unless he likes her."

What about now, Hank? What do you feel about me now? I know you like me—but how much?

Clumsily, I plunged ahead. "You always

seem so—I don't know—kind of distant when we're together. Not like now. When we're talking like this it feels OK—" I was in over my head now, but I couldn't seem to stop babbling. It was like one of those dreams where you're running and running and not getting anywhere. In fact, I swore I could feel Hank drawing away from me.

There was a rumble as he cleared his throat. Then his voice seemed to go up a few octaves—sounding strangely unlike Hank.

"I—I thought we were getting along pretty well. I like you, Mattie. I like you a lot. The truth is, I never counted on liking you this much."

There. It was out. But instead of feeling good about it, I felt lousy—as if I'd trapped him into saying something he wasn't ready for. Clearly, he was as embarrassed about the whole thing as I was.

"I'm sorry, Hank," I said. "I didn't mean to put you on the spot."

"Hey, that's OK." His voice cracked, then lowered again to its former throatiness. "I'm sorry, too."

"What for?"

"I don't know. For being too big a dope to figure out what was bothering you."

"I don't think you're a dope. Remember," I added, hoping to strike a lighter note, "you're supposed to be irresistible."

"Right." He laughed. "In that case, would you consider going to the dance with me?"

"Yes, definitely."

"Great." I could hear him sigh, as if he were relieved.

Long after we'd hung up, I lay on my bed in the darkness, going over everything we'd said and wondering what I'd wear to the dance.

Chapter Seven

"Well—how do I look?"

Nita twirled before us in her haute couture creation: a long, sleek gown of midnight-blue crepe de chine, with billowy sleeves and a scooped neckline embroidered with tiny beads. I had to admit it was stunning. But the transformation of my sister was what surprised me the most.

"You look like a different person," I told her.

She'd pinned her hair on top of her head so that a few tendrils escaped down her neck. The new hairstyle, along with her makeup, made her look at least four years older. It was the first time I'd ever seen Nita as a grown-up person instead of just my gawky kid sister. I actually felt drab beside her in my plaid skirt and blouse.

Nita planted her hands on her hips. "I hope that's supposed to be a compliment."

"Don't worry—it is. A definite improvement over the old you."

"You look beautiful, baby," commented Dad, getting up from his armchair to kiss her cheek. "A real 'ten' in my book. And a real winner, no matter what happens at the judging."

Nita was positively glowing. "Mom helped me pick out the material, but I did all the rest myself."

It had taken nearly two hours at the fabric store in Seattle for her to get everything she wanted, including the two different patterns she'd worked her design from. Mom and Nita never got bored shopping for clothes and material—they're alike in that way. I, on the other hand, would just as soon get shopping over with as quickly as possible. Trying on clothes is not my idea of a good time.

Lunch made up for it, though. Instead of

the Sheraton, Mom took us to a French restaurant where we gorged on crab salad, quiche, and chocolate mousse. Nita groaned all the way home, saying she wouldn't be able to fit into her dress when it was finished.

All in all, it was a special day—the kind that reminded me of how things used to be B.D.: Before the Divorce. Only for some reason, it didn't make me sad the way it would have a year before. I guess that's part of growing up—learning that people going their separate ways isn't necessarily bad.

"We'd better hurry if we want to get seats near the front," said Barb as she finished wrestling Zac into a pair of quilted overalls. "It's getting late."

"Yeah," twittered Nita. "I hear Mary Lou Jenkins is doing a belly-dance routine for her talent number. We don't want to be late for *that!*"

The pageant was the event that kicked off the Winter Festival. The next day, Saturday, were the sled races and snow sculpture contest, topped off by the big dance that night. One year, I remember, we didn't have enough snow, and a bunch of men with dump trucks drove up into the mountains and brought back a huge pile of it. Needless to say, Port Kearney is big on tradition. Linda and I entered ourselves in the junior team division of the sculpture contest. Our sculpture was to be "Garfield the Snow-Cat."

Despite some confusion when Nita caught her hem in the car door and had to run back inside for a few repair stitches, we arrived in plenty of time. Dad and Barb went off in search of seats while Nita and I made our way backstage amid a jungle of crepe paper and general confusion.

"I think I'm going to be sick," Nita said, moaning and clutching my arm with sweaty fingers. "I've never been so nervous in my whole life!"

"You'll be fine," I reassured her. "All you've got to do is walk out there and look gorgeous. Mom was right about the dress. It's original. Judges always count high for originality."

She stopped chewing her lip. "You're not just saying that to make me feel better?"

"Cross my heart." I traced my finger across my chest. "When have I ever lied to you?"

She thought for a moment, then asked, "What about that time you told me I would get square eyes from watching too much TV?"

We both laughed, breaking some of the tension. I glanced around and caught the eye of Cheryl Abramson, a girl I knew slightly from my PE class. She waved, then went back to trilling on her flute. Another girl, dressed in a striped leotard, was practicing her gymnastics routine on a balance beam. She'd fallen off twice, and I could see that she was close to tears. I counted three baton twirlers and two girls clutching piano sheet music like me. I didn't really count, since I wasn't competing, but they must not have known that because I caught them whispering and glancing at me with nervous expressions.

Nita came on fifth, right after Mary Lou's belly dance, which nearly brought the house down as well as raising a few eyebrows. Then the spotlight was on Nita. She looked cool and elegant as she glided out from the wings to my accompaniment of the theme from *Chariots of Fire*. When she reached center stage, she twirled dramatically.

"There you have it," crowed Mrs. Blanchard, our French teacher, who was the emcee for the evening. Her accent lent an air of glamour to the event, I thought. "A Nita Winston original! Isn't she lovely? Let's give her a big hand!"

The audience applauded enthusiastically, to which Nita responded with a gracefully executed curtsy. I was glad the piano was partially hidden behind the curtain so I wouldn't have to do the same.

An hour and a half later, following a parade of the girls wearing their formals, the judges announced their decision. Cheryl Abramson had won the title of Miss Winter Festival, mostly because of a flawless flute rendition of "Annie's Song," I suspected, but Nita had gotten first runner-up!

Everyone rushed up to congratulate the winners. Barb threw her arms around Nita, and kissed her on both cheeks. Nita looked as though she were still in a state of shock.

Tears glistened in Barbara's eyes as she said, "You were so beautiful! As graceful as any swan!" Then she beamed at me. "And, Mattie, you were wonderful, too. I was so proud—of both of you."

Unwittingly Nita spoiled the moment by asking, "Where's Mom? She said she would be here."

Dad got that uncomfortable look he always gets when the subject of his former wife comes up. "I'm sure your mother—" he started to say.

"I'm sure she felt terrible that she couldn't make it," Barb cut in hurriedly. "But—she sent you this so you'd know she was thinking of you."

From the depths of Zac's diaper bag, she produced a square florist's box containing a pale lavender orchid corsage. She made a fuss of pinning the fragile blossom onto Nita's shoulder.

"There—isn't it pretty? It goes perfectly with your formal."

I glanced over at my stepmother in surprise. I knew Mom hadn't sent the corsage because I'd seen the florist's receipt on Barb's dresser that afternoon. Why had she lied?

Then, suddenly, it all made sense. Barb knew how much Nita had counted on Mom's being there that night. I was sure Mom had a good excuse—she's always having last-minute emergencies at work that make her forget the time. But Nita would have been crushed if it hadn't been for the unexpected remembrance of the corsage—a gift that Barb had intended to give herself.

But she'd ended up giving my sister something far more valuable.

It was silly, I know, but all of a sudden I was on the verge of crying. As soon as Nita was out of earshot, swept away by a tide of giggling girlfriends, I wanted to tell Barb how I felt about what she'd done. But the words wouldn't come. The emotion was just too big.

When Hank called later that night, I confided the incident to him. "Why couldn't I say something to her?" I asked. "Why is it so difficult?"

"Opening up is always hard. I know. I feel that way myself a lot of the time. Even when it's something good, you're afraid of getting hurt."

"But that's dumb, isn't it?"

"Yeah, really dumb. But I guess people should say dumb things more often. Maybe they'd find out they weren't so dumb after all."

Strangely enough, it made sense. "I know exactly what you mean."

"It's like when you're learning to skate and you keep falling down at first. I remember I really felt like an idiot. I didn't think I'd ever be any good. But it got easier after a while."

"Somehow, I just can't imagine you falling down."

"I guess I'll have to show you my scars to prove it."

"Watch out or they may become part of Port Kearney's Hall of Fame," I said, referring to the glass trophy case in which Coach Benson had crammed a mountain of memorabilia, including his own football helmet from high school.

Hank laughed. "You're crazy, Mattie Winston. Absolutely nuts. I never thought I'd meet anyone as crazy as me. You're an all-time first."

My skin prickled at the way he'd said it. "So are you," I confessed softly. *The first boy I ever felt that close to.*

Did that mean I was in love?

Probably.

Suddenly I didn't care anymore if he knew. "I guess falling in love with someone is a little like learning how to skate," I blurted out. "Scary—but nice."

"Are you scared now?" he asked huskily.

"No. Not now. Not when it's like this."

"I wish . . ." His voice trailed into silence.

"You wish what?"

"I wish it could always be this way."

"Why can't it?"

"I don't know. Things always seem to get in the way. But I want you to know something—right now—in case I lose my nerve later on. *I think I love you.* Wow—" He emitted a shaky laugh. "Now I know what you mean about being scared."

I caught a glimpse of myself in the large round mirror that hung over my vanity table. My hair was a mess, my face was flushed pink, and I was grinning like an idiot.

"I wish I could be with you right now," Hank said.

"No, you don't!" I shrieked. "I'm a mess. Wait until tomorrow night. I promise I won't disappoint you then."

Dreamily I imagined myself hand in hand with Hank, the two of us gliding effortlessly onto the dance floor. *The music begins, a soft romantic number. Hank looks at me, his eyes filled with love. He smiles, drawing me into his arms so that my head nes-*

tles in the cove between his chest and shoulder. We fall in step with the music. . . .

  "Tomorrow—right," Hank said, bringing me back to earth. He took a deep breath. "Listen, Mattie, I've gotta go. I hear my dad coming. He doesn't like me to stay on the phone too long, and believe me, the Incredible Hulk's wrath is nothing compared to his." His voice dropped to an even lower whisper than usual. "Bye—I meant what I said before: I love you."

  "I love you, too." But I'd spoken too late. He'd already hung up.

Chapter Eight

"I just adore your dress, Mattie," said Janine when I saw her at the dance. "Did you make it yourself?"

"Sorry," I told her. "You've got the wrong sister. I'm a lousy seamstress."

"I remember—you played the piano at the pageant. Hey, you were really good." She turned to Jay beside her. "Didn't you think so, Jay?"

Jay nodded, his eyes flickering over me. "Yeah." I wondered what he thought of me then.

I was wearing a ruffled peach-colored

formal in a silky fabric that fluttered about my ankles as I walked. It wasn't as low-cut or form-fitting as Janine's stylish metallic-blue sheath, but I thought I looked terrific anyway. I had coiled my hair up on top of my head, crowning it with a wreath of tiny silk flowers. Hank had whistled when he arrived at the door to pick me up.

"I looked for you at the snow sculpture contest," I told him when Jay and Janine had drifted off in the direction of the refreshment table.

Linda and I had placed third with our "Garfield the Snow-Cat," even though he came out slightly lopsided after the sun had gone to work on him. First prize in the junior division had gone, deservedly, to John Bellesario, the artist who had done the Winter Festival posters as well. His sculpture of a beautifully detailed sperm whale occupied half the town plaza when it was finished. He called it "Snowby Dick."

"I had to stick around the house and help my dad with some stuff," Hank explained.

"Gee, that was too bad. You missed all the fun when Corky Connors and Jennifer

Newman got into a fight with the snowballs from her Pac-Man sculpture." I laughed. "Poor Pac-Man was the one who got eaten this time."

"I wish I'd been there."

"Well, I'm glad you're here *now*." Smiling, I slipped my arm through his. I thought how handsome Hank looked in his powder-blue tuxedo jacket. It set off the blue of his eyes.

The music was playing. We moved onto the dance floor, guided by the beat. Cotton snow, huge paper snowflakes, and purple tree cutouts had transformed the auditorium into a winter wonderland. Pale violet light flooded the dance floor, sparkling off the glitter ball that hung from the ceiling.

Linda sailed past in Glenn's arms. She looked like a fairy princess in a dress of billowy pale pink chiffon, a red rose pinned in her hair.

"Hi, you two," she called. "How's it going?"

I gave her a thumbs-up sign.

Spotting Nita and Ken, I waved, but my sister—dressed in the gown she'd designed for the pageant—was oblivious. Apparently she and Ken had discovered that there were other ways of communicating besides conversation.

Halfway through the evening, Ginger Welles, a friend of mine who was our junior class president, got up on stage and announced that the next dance would be the "Mix-and-Match." Everyone had been given a number on a slip of paper at the door: blue for the boys, pink for the girls. We were to be paired at random, a tradition that often resulted in some strange couples, like the time five-foot-four Randy Webber got stuck with five-eleven Brenda Carpenter at the Christmas dance.

I stood by as Hank was towed off by a delighted Jeanette Porter. Then my number was called. I stepped up to meet the boy who held the corresponding number nineteen—but the second I saw who he was, I wanted to run and hide.

Standing before me was Jay Thompson.

We looked at each other in embarrassment. Stiffly he took my hand and led me onto the dance floor. I noticed his palm was sweaty. I felt numb. Neither of us had spoken a word to the other, and the silence stretched between us like an Arctic glacier.

Then Jay smiled at me. Up close, I saw that his brown eyes were shot with splinters of lighter gold. *He's really cute when he smiles,* I thought.

They were playing the theme from *Endless Love.* Almost imperceptibly, I felt Jay begin to relax as our bodies picked up the slow rhythm. He was shorter than Hank, only slightly taller than I, so our shoulders nearly met as we danced. Jay was a good dancer, I noted.

I was actually enjoying myself.

Jay must have felt the same, for suddenly he drew me in closer, his arm encircling my waist. I could feel the warm, damp pressure of his hand through the thin fabric of my dress. His breath ruffled the hair just over my left ear. An odd tingly feeling started at the back of my neck and worked its way down my spine.

Then abruptly the dance was over, and we broke apart. The spell was gone, leaving me to wonder if I had imagined the whole thing.

"Thanks," Jay muttered, flashing me that quicksilver smile before moving off in search of Janine.

Hank caught up with me by the refreshment table. "Whew!" he gasped. "That Jeanette had me in a clinch I thought I'd never get out of!"

Gratefully I snuggled against him, pushing Jay to the back of my mind.

Chapter Nine

It was mid-March when Hank dropped his bombshell. We were sitting out on the sun porch that overlooks our backyard. The snow had all melted away, and new grass had begun to push up among the dry, brown stalks of winter. It looked as though we'd have an early spring.

"My dad was offered a job in New York," Hank said, carefully avoiding my eyes.

I sat up in my chair. "He's not going to take it, is he?"

"He has to." Hank sighed in resignation. "Things haven't been too good lately, and we really need the money."

My heart froze. "Does that mean—" I couldn't force the words out.

"Yeah—looks like we'll have to move." Hank supplied the dreaded words for me, finally allowing himself to look at me. I could see that he was upset and was trying hard not to show it.

I felt as if someone had come along and slammed a door in my face, leaving me alone and cold on the outside. These last two months Hank and I had grown so close. Now he was telling me it was over, or it might as well be with three thousand miles between us. *Just when it was really beginning . . .*

I thought of the nights I'd poured out my thoughts and secret dreams to Hank, mostly over the phone, where we did our best talking. I thought of the long, quiet Saturday afternoons we'd spent walking through the countryside or just being comfortable together.

I couldn't believe I was losing Hank—my first really special boyfriend.

Hot tears blurred my vision. "When?" I asked in a small voice.

"Soon," Hank replied miserably. "Mom's already started putting stuff in boxes. It'll probably be in a couple of weeks."

A couple of weeks! I longed for Hank to put his arms around me, to tell me he would always love me no matter what. But Hank only sat there with that terrible helpless expression, staring off into space.

"I know how you feel," commiserated Linda when I told her later on that afternoon.

"No, you don't," I wailed, ignoring the fact that she was only trying to make me feel better. "You've still got Glenn!"

"That's true. But I can imagine how I *would* feel if Glenn had to move away."

"It's awful! I'll never see him again!"

"You could always write," she offered.

"I know, but somehow it's not the same." I slumped down on the carpet beside her bed. "Do you realize how far it is from here to New York? *Three thousand miles.*"

"Gosh, Mattie, that *is* a long way. Poor Hank—he must be feeling pretty awful about it, too."

"You know Hank. He doesn't show his feelings much. He was pretty quiet about the whole thing, actually."

"You know what they say—still waters run deep."

"It just makes me want to scream. He didn't even tell me he was going to miss me!"

Thoughtfully Linda stroked the nubby ear of her old stuffed dog, Dobie. "Maybe he doesn't want to make it any worse than it already is."

"How could it be any worse?" I wanted to know. "We're never going to see each other again!"

"That's not necessarily true. He could always come out for a visit."

"When? In five years? Come on, Linda, be sensible. Hank might as well be living on the moon as far as I'm concerned."

"Well, there's no use moping about it yet. You still have a couple of weeks." She grabbed my hand, pulling me to my feet. "Come on, let's get something to eat. Food always makes me feel better when I'm miserable."

I shook my head. "Are you kidding? I couldn't eat a bite. In fact, I may never eat again."

Poor thing—she died of a broken heart, they would say at my funeral. *She couldn't eat. She just wasted away to nothing. So young—such a terrible, terrible tragedy. . . .*

"There's a gallon of butterscotch pecan in the freezer, and my mom won't be back until six," she coaxed, giving me a devilish look.

I sighed. "Maybe just a spoonful. . . ."

An hour and two gigantic bowls of ice cream later, I somehow felt better. How could anyone who was dying of a broken heart be so disgustingly ravenous? I wondered.

"Look at it this way," said Linda, licking the last drop of butterscotch pecan from her spoon. "I know it's not the same, but he could still call you once in a while."

"That's true," I said, sniffing. "I suppose it's better than nothing, isn't it?" I knew I was grasping at straws, but I didn't care.

"I'm going to miss you, Mattie." Hank's voice sounded strained.

"Me, too. A lot." My own voice sounded small and faraway as I responded, clutching the phone. "Will you write sometimes?"

"I'll try," he said. "I'm not very good at writing, you know. But," he added wistfully,

"I'll be thinking about you. You can count on that."

"Yeah—same here." I drew in a deep, shaky breath. "Well, at least you'll still be able to play hockey. I hear they're big on hockey in the East." I wanted to cheer him up before we both started bawling.

"Let's hope so. It won't be easy getting used to a new school, though. Especially since I'm coming in so late in the year."

"You'll do fine," I told him. "You're irresistible, remember? I'll bet you'll have girls crawling all over you after the first week."

"There's only one girl I'm interested in."

"Oh?" I laughed in spite of the tears that were rolling down my cheeks. "And who might she be?"

"Well—maybe you know her. She's got this long blond hair, you see—kind of a golden color. Her eyes are blue, actually sort of a blue-gray, but really beautiful. And she's got this really dynamite smile. Oh, and a few freckles. She hates her freckles, but I think they're adorable. Any clues so far?"

I giggled. "She sounds vaguely familiar."

"That's another thing—she doesn't think she's all that pretty, but let me tell you, she's one in a million. Janine Hawes couldn't even come close to her."

"I wouldn't let Janine hear you say that," I warned. "She thinks she's the best-looking girl in school."

"She's all right, but her nose doesn't wrinkle when she laughs, for one thing."

"You like girls with wrinkly noses?"

"Don't forget freckles."

"She sounds ravishing," I said, deadpan.

Hank cracked up, and suddenly I was laughing and crying at the same time. Tears were pouring down my cheeks, and my nose was a mess. I realized that one of the things I would miss most about him was his nutty sense of humor.

"Her name is Mattie Winston," Hank said, "and when you see her, will you tell her something for me?"

"What?"

"Tell her I love her. It's important she knows, you see, because after I move it'll probably be a long time before I see her again."

"I don't think I'll have to tell her," I answered softly. "I think she already knows."

*　　*　　*

Hank stood on my front porch, hands shoved into the pockets of his Levis, looking like someone whose dog had just been run over. I was trying hard not to cry.

"Are you sure you don't want to come inside?" I asked, making a feeble attempt to sound normal. "I could make us some cocoa."

"Naw—I can't stay. The moving guys finished loading up this morning. We're supposed to take off in a few minutes, so I don't have much time."

Tears filled my eyes, and I made no effort to blink them back. "I guess this is it, huh?"

Hank nodded miserably. "Mattie, I—" he seemed to choke on his words. He spread his hands helplessly, as if to say that what he was feeling was too big to express.

"I know, Hank," I whispered, burrowing against the solid wall of his chest as his arms folded about me. "Me, too."

We stood there for a long moment, arms wrapped around each other, before Hank reluctantly drew away.

"I've got to go, Mattie," he murmured hoarsely. "Mom and Dad'll kill me if I'm late."

"Goodbye, Hank." It was just one word,

one lousy little word, but it was the hardest word I'd ever had to say. "Write me?"

"Yeah, sure. I'll do my best. It's just that—" He shrugged, offering me an apologetic grimace. "Well, you know I'm not much with words." He brushed my chin with his knuckles. I could see his Adam's apple working up and down, as if he were trying not to cry, too. "You better believe I'll be thinking about you, though."

"Me, too," I answered lamely.

He kissed me one last time, fiercely, then turned to go, quickly walking down the front steps to his car. He kept his head bowed and didn't look back. Then, as he got into his car, he did look up, smiled quickly, and brushed a tear from the corner of his eye.

"Goodbye. I'll miss you," I croaked, as his car disappeared around the corner.

Chapter Ten

I read an article in *Seventeen* once, all about getting over a broken heart. It listed a lot of "don'ts": don't gorge yourself on junk food; don't hole up in your room; don't listen to soppy love songs; don't spend hours staring at his picture; and don't spend your time wondering what he's doing right now.

In the first week after Hank left, I was guilty of almost all of these "don'ts." I ate an entire medium-sized pizza in one sitting. I spent a whole afternoon holed up in my room listening to soppy love songs and wondering what he was doing. The only thing I didn't do was stare at his picture, since I didn't have one.

Hank had written to me only once so far—a postcard of the Empire State Building. "Hi!" he had scribbled across the back. "A big city, but not as bad as I expected. Hope all is well back in P.K. Love, Hank."

"Not a single 'I miss you,' " I complained to Linda as she helped me pull weeds in the front yard on Saturday.

"Maybe he was afraid your father would read it," Linda reasoned.

"Maybe it's because he doesn't miss me." I was already beginning to wonder if I'd imagined all those nice things he'd told me before he left.

Linda jabbed her spade into the soft earth. "Do *you* miss Hank?"

I stared at her in astonishment. "How can you even ask? Of course I miss him!"

"OK, OK—don't bite my head off. I was just wondering, that's all."

"*Obviously*, you don't know what it's like to suffer," I informed her coldly.

"Oh, come on," she said as she pushed a stray curl from her eyes. "You don't have to get mad. It's just that—well, I was wondering if you ever figured out which Hank you were in love with—Dr. Jekyll or Mr. Hyde."

"Uh-oh, you're not going to start that split personality stuff again. OK, so Hank is a little hard to get to know on the surface, but once you dig down to the middle, he's a real softie."

Linda giggled. "Sounds like biting into a Mallomar."

I shot her a look of utter disgust. "You can joke all you want. Just don't come running to me if Glenn ever tells you he's moving to Timbuktu."

Linda came over and put her arms around me. "I'm sorry, Mattie. I didn't mean to make you feel bad. I really do sympathize. It's just—don't you think you ought to try and get out more? Have fun, meet other boys?"

"It's only been a week."

"I know. I'm not telling you to forget Hank. Just don't *enshrine* him. Look at you—you haven't worn a drop of makeup since he left!"

I had to admit she was right. I did look a mess. And moping around certainly wasn't going to bring Hank back. Also, I had to admit that maybe I *was* overdoing the martyr bit just a touch.

"OK, OK," I said. "Will it make you happier if I put on green eyeshadow?"

Linda laughed. "Never mind. I can see I opened the wrong can of worms. But," she added, "there's still the problem of how to cheer you up. You can't sit around the house forever. Remember, *he's* up there with King Kong, and you're still stuck in good old boring Port Kearney."

"Thanks for the reminder," I said. "What exactly did you have in mind?"

She thought for a moment. "How about a slumber party? We haven't had one in ages—it might be fun." She started laughing. "Remember the time we put Lori Boudacoff's bra in the freezer? Then she put it in the dryer, and it shrank?"

"Yeah—and she was mad because it fit better shrunk."

"I don't think she ever forgave us!"

We both collapsed into giggles. Suddenly I felt nostalgic for those uncomplicated days before boys entered the picture. I knew there was no turning back—and I didn't want to, not really—but I couldn't help recalling how much simpler life was then. The idea of having a slumber party like the ones we used to have in junior high appealed to me.

"I sometimes think boys are more trouble than they're worth," said Sueann Helms, who was currently wallowing in misery over the umpteenth break-up with her boyfriend, Curt.

The sentiment was seconded by Ginger. "You're absolutely right—but where would we be without them?"

"Yeah," Linda said. "Kissing is no fun when you do it alone." She emphasized her point by snatching up a throw pillow from the couch and smothering it with kisses.

We all collapsed onto our sleeping bags in hilarity. I wasn't sure if my stomach hurt from laughing so much or whether it was all the food we'd eaten. So far, the five of us, including Nita, had managed to consume two giant-sized pizzas, three bags of potato chips, and an entire platter of homemade fudge.

"What's it like when Glenn kisses you?" asked Nita. I knew she was wondering because Ken still hadn't worked up the nerve to kiss her, only she didn't want to admit it and seem inexperienced around us older girls.

"Like heaven," Linda said, cooing.

"In that case," said Ginger, nibbling on the last piece of fudge, "I think you're being selfish. If Glenn's kisses are so heavenly, you ought to let us sample a few."

"Sorry, girls, but Glenn's lips are off limits to anyone but me."

"Do we have to talk about kissing?" Sueann asked. "It makes me think of Curt, and I'd rather stay mad at him, if you don't mind."

Ginger tossed a potato chip at her. "Admit it, Sueann. You can't stay mad at Curt for more than five minutes."

"OK—I confess. I'm still crazy about him. But I'd jump in front of a speeding train before I'd admit it to Curt."

"Why?" I asked. "If that's the way you feel. Isn't it better to be honest?"

"Honesty isn't always the name of the game when it comes to love," she said. "You've heard that old saying, 'All's fair in love and war,' haven't you?"

I wondered if Hank had been honest with me when he told me he loved me. I was beginning to doubt it. Nearly two weeks, and he'd only sent me that one postcard! Wouldn't he have written a letter or at least called if he really cared?

That was what I missed most—his calls. Already the image of Hank himself was rapidly fading. Whenever I tried to conjure up the memory of his kisses, I got a fuzzy picture of Hank bending over me, blue eyes intent on my face, but all I could remember was that he kissed with his eyes open.

Thinking back, I wasn't sure I would ever have described Hank's kisses as "heavenly." Or was Linda simply exaggerating about Glenn? Did all boys kiss pretty much alike? So far, I hadn't met one who really stood out from the rest.

Unless there was something wrong with me.

Was it, as Linda once said, just that I was unlucky where love was concerned?

"Let's face it," said Ginger, echoing my thoughts. "We're all doomed as far as men are concerned. Doomed if we do and doomed if we don't."

Her latest witticism was greeted by a burst of laughter. We were making so much noise that Barb was forced to make an appearance, warning us that if we woke up the baby, he'd be on our hands for the rest of the night. Her gaze swept over the clutter of plates, crumpled napkins, and empty soda cans that littered the living room carpet, but with her usual tact, she refrained from making any comment.

"Good night, girls," she called before disappearing up the staircase. "Try not to have *too* much fun."

"I know," whispered Nita. "Let's turn out the lights and tell spooky stories."

Linda jumped up and began switching off lights. It was the moment she'd been waiting for. "I know one that'll fry your hair," she said. "Have you ever heard the one about The Poisoned Purple Crib?" It didn't matter if we had or not—she was going to tell it anyway.

I snuggled down in my sleeping bag, mildly surprised to realize that, Hank or no Hank, I was having a good time.

Chapter Eleven

Sunday morning Nita and I stayed home to clean up the mess left by the slumber party while Dad and Barb went into town for gardening supplies. Both of them are gardening nuts; in fact, that's how they met—at a rose show in Seattle, where Barb had her White Star entered. As she likes to tell it, she didn't take home the blue ribbon, but Dad was an even better prize.

I was immersed to my elbows in soapy water when the phone rang. My heart leaped. *Please let it be Hank*, I always prayed, annoyed when it turned out to be one of Nita's gabby friends or a business call for Dad. Trailing soapsuds across the linoleum, I went to answer it, picking it up on the third ring.

"Is Dr. Winston there?" an excited-sounding male voice asked. For some reason he sounded vaguely familiar.

"No, he's not," I answered, my heart plunging back to earth. I tried not to let my disappointment show. "Have you tried the emergency number at his office? There should be someone there who can help you."

"I already tried. I can't get an answer—and this sure is an emergency. My mare got her leg caught in a barbed-wire fence. I cut her free with wire clippers, but she's so panicked, I can't see how badly she's injured. But there's a lot of blood." He sounded very upset.

"Is there someone there who can help you until my father gets back?" I asked.

"That's just the trouble. I'm the only one home right now. Listen—I've got to get back and see if—"

"Wait a minute," I broke in impulsively. "Why don't I come out? I've worked with my father before, so I might be able to help. I'll bring the first-aid kit."

"I won't argue with you. I could sure use the help." He gave me the address, which was only a few miles outside of town.

Scribbling a quick note to Dad, I left Nita with instructions to give it to him when he got home so he'd know where to find me. I grabbed the keys to Barb's VW. I knew she wouldn't mind my using it without her permission since it was an emergency.

I found the address easily. It was an old-style frame house set in a green elbow between two hills. There was a barn in back, and I could see cattle grazing in the distance.

A jean-clad figure waved to me from the fence that separated the pasture from the road. I could see from the way the injured horse was jerking her head that he was having trouble keeping her calm. Snatching up the first-aid kit, I ran toward him, glad I'd remembered to wear my old rubber boots as I plowed through the muck of the pasture.

A jolt of recognition zapped me when I got near enough to see who the boy was. "J-Jay?" I stammered. "Why didn't you tell me it was you?"

"Would you have come if you'd known? I'm sorry, Mattie. I know this must seem like one more reason to hate me, but I couldn't take the chance."

He regarded me unflinchingly from under the battered brim of an old cowboy hat. His mouth was set in a grim line, but only because he was worried about his horse, a pretty chestnut mare, who tossed her head nervously as I approached her.

"Never mind about all that," I said, masking my unease with a cool, businesslike attitude. "I think we'd better get her into the barn. Then we can clean off the blood and take a look at her leg."

After we got the mare into her stall, I washed off the blood while Jay stroked her neck to calm her. Fortunately her injuries were minor. I dabbed antiseptic on the cuts and then wrapped the leg in a bandage. "You should still have my father look at this," I cautioned. "I'm not exactly a licensed veterinarian, you know."

"Maybe not," Jay said. "But I don't know what I would have done without you."

I blushed, fumbling with the latch on the first-aid kit so he wouldn't see how uncomfortable I felt around him. There was something about Jay—something about his voice that disturbed me, though I couldn't put my finger on the reason.

We stood in the semidarkness of the barn, near the stall where the mare stood happily munching on an unexpected treat of a bucket of alfalfa and molasses. Jay was wearing an old pair of Levis faded to snow white at the knees and a denim shirt rolled up at the elbows to reveal his muscular forearms. He regarded me with a strangely intense look that caused a shiver to dart up the back of my neck.

"Look, Mattie," he said in a soft, hushed voice, "I know what you must think of me, and I want to apologize."

Suddenly I knew why Jay's voice had sounded so familiar to me. Suddenly I knew why he had been avoiding me for so long. There was no mistaking that huskily lowered tone—*Jay was the voice on the telephone!* He was the one who had been calling me all that time, pretending to be Hank. *He* was Hank's alter-ego!

My senses spun with the realization. I felt all the blood drain from my face, leaving me cold and numb. I wanted to run away, but I could only stand there, staring at Jay in horror as if he'd suddenly sprouted two horns and a tail.

Why? I wanted to know. Had it all been some sort of sick joke cooked up by the two of them to make a fool of me? In one big humiliating rush, I remembered all the things I'd told Jay in confidence, thinking all the time that I'd been confiding them to Hank. *I told him I loved him*, I realized with a sick feeling in the pit of my stomach.

"You—" I managed to choke past the lump in my throat. I was afraid I was going to cry at any moment. "*It was you on the phone!*"

"Please, Mattie, let me explain—" His arms reached toward me, but I shrank back, not wanting him to touch me, not wanting my body to betray me as it had once before at the dance.

"Don't bother," I told him coldly. "I think I already understand. You and Hank must have thought it was pretty funny—how easy it was to fool me. I admit I was stupid to believe all those lies you told me." Hot tears spilled down my cheeks. I brushed them away, angry with myself for letting Jay see how much he'd hurt me.

But Jay didn't look smug. Actually, I had to admit, he looked pretty miserable himself.

"It wasn't like that, Mattie. In the beginning, I'll admit I was just doing it as a favor to Hank. But after a while things just sort of got out of hand. I couldn't stop—" He swallowed hard. "I found out I liked you too much."

"What about Hank?" I demanded. "How could you let me think he was in love with me?" I couldn't bring myself to add the words, *or that I was in love with him?*

"Hank cared about you," Jay said. "That's what made it so confusing. I don't know if I can explain it right—but you see, he's always had this problem talking to girls. He gets all tied up in knots, especially when it's someone he really likes. You were someone he really liked, and he didn't want to blow it this time, so he begged me to call you and pretend I was him. Just once, he said, just to ask you out. We both have pretty deep voices, so we figured that bit about not wanting to talk too loud would work."

"Well, it did—are you satisfied? You just should have quit while you were ahead!"

"I wanted to—at first. But Hank kept insisting. He'd done me a lot of favors, so I

116

said OK, even though I felt rotten about fooling you like that. So I'd call you up, then I'd have to remember everything we talked about so I could tell Hank later on."

"Everything?"

He blushed. "Well—not exactly. A lot of the stuff we talked about was too private. I realized after a while that even though I was pretending to be Hank, I liked you, too—for—for myself. Only, of course, I couldn't tell Hank. He's my best friend."

"So I got stuck right in the middle. Tell me something, Jay, did Hank ever *really* love me?"

"Yes, he did. But I guess he just didn't know how to say it."

"Thanks," I flung at him, "for bothering to explain it all. Maybe someday I'll be grateful to you."

I started to walk away, but Jay's arms shot out, capturing me against the hard wall of his chest. "Wait, Mattie," he murmured in that same husky, emotional voice that had once filled me with such warmth. "I want you to know, I meant all those things I said. I was speaking for me, not Hank, when I said them. Believe me."

Why should I believe you? a voice inside me screamed. Why should I believe Jay when he'd tricked me—lied to me? I struggled to free myself from his embrace, but he only held me tighter. Suddenly his lips were pressing down on my mouth. I stopped fighting him, aware only of the fiery sensations that were washing over me, melting my anger.

"Oh, Mattie," he murmured thickly, brushing his fingertips across my cheek. "I've wanted to do that for a long time." He found my lips again in a long tender kiss that was even more passionate than the first.

My knees were the consistency of warm butter. I couldn't move. I could hardly think. And I was so confused—I didn't know what my feelings were anymore. Part of me wanted Jay to go on holding me, kissing me, but at the same time I couldn't forget what he'd done. After all the lies, could I believe what he was telling me? Could I ever trust him?

"I—I have to go now," I stammered, abruptly wrenching free.

Jay called after me as I ran across the yard, but I wouldn't stop. I was afraid even to look back. Tears momentarily blinded me as I fumbled for the keys. I brushed them away with my fist and started the engine. A glance in the rearview mirror revealed Jay's forlorn figure standing in the driveway, shading his eyes against the sun as he watched me drive away. The image tugged at my heart, even as I told myself I never wanted to see Jay Thompson again as long as I lived.

Chapter Twelve

"Mattie—what's wrong?" Barb took one look at me and set down the flat of peonies she was carrying on the back step.

"I—oh, everything," I said, bursting into tears.

Barb put an arm around my shoulders and led me over to the chaise longue. "Is it Hank?" she asked.

"Sort of." I poured out the entire story while Barb listened in sympathetic surprise. "Isn't that the most disgusting thing you've ever heard?"

"It is—strange," she agreed, "but people often do strange things when they're in love."

"Do you really think he loves me?" I asked, blowing into the tissue she'd dug out of her apron pocket.

"Who?" she asked. "Hank or Jay?"

Without a moment's hesitation, I answered, "Jay, of course."

Barb cupped her hand under my chin, tilting it back to meet her penetrating gaze. "I think you already know the answer to that, don't you?"

I hugged her, brimming over with a sudden appreciation of all the ways in which Barbara had been there for both Nita and me when we really needed someone to talk to and understand us. She would never take Mom's place, but then, she didn't really have to. Barb had carved out a special place in our family that was all her own.

"I love you," I blurted out. There, it was out. And it had been so easy. Why had I been so afraid to say it before?

Barb had tears in her eyes, too. "I know, Mattie, and I love you, too."

"Why is it so hard for people to say that

to each other?" I wondered out loud. "Why do we have to wear so many masks? Why can't we just be honest?"

"Because loving hurts sometimes." Barb smiled. "But if we don't open ourselves up, if we don't allow ourselves to get hurt once in a while, then none of the good things can get in, either. I think," she added thoughtfully, "that it might have been easier for Jay to tell you what was in his heart while he was pretending to be someone else."

I shook my head. "I'm so confused. I *thought* Hank was the one I loved, but if Hank was really Jay, then—" I couldn't bring myself to say it.

"Don't worry." Barb patted my shoulder. "It'll all make sense to you if you give yourself time. Where love is concerned, things have a way of working themselves out for the best."

I wasn't so sure about that, but I didn't say so. I didn't want to hurt her feelings by asking her how she could possibly know about that sort of thing. Her relationship with Dad seemed so easy and uncomplicated.

"I'll tell you something I've never told anyone else," she confided. "When your father and I were engaged, I nearly called the whole thing off once."

"Why?" I wanted to know.

"It all seems so silly now, but at the time— well, I knew how you girls felt about me, and I wasn't so sure I was doing the right thing, trying to fill your mother's place. Now I know that no one can ever really take anyone else's place."

"In other words, Jay never *really* took Hank's place, even when he thought he had?"

"Something like that." She nodded.

"So you think I should give him a second chance?"

"You're the only one who can answer that, Mattie."

Except that I couldn't answer it right then. I was still such a tangle of emotions—I was angry, upset, confused—and, yes, I had to admit I was attracted to Jay as well. I couldn't forget the feel of his arms around me, the touch of his lips. . . .

I was hoping it would all work itself out as Barb had predicted, but I wasn't so sure it would. No one I knew had ever been faced with a situation as crazy as this. It was like a play we'd read in English. *Cyrano de Bergerac*. It was about a guy who was really crazy about a girl named Roxanne. He was handsome, but he didn't know how to talk to women so he got his ugly friend with a big nose to write really incredible love letters, which he signed his name to. I couldn't remember how it had ended, but I didn't think it was happily. . . .

"Well." Barb stood up, brushing the wrinkles from her skirt. "What do you say we get these peonies into the ground before they all wilt?"

That night at dinner, I could only pick at my food, though it was one of my favorite meals: roast leg of lamb with mint jelly, new potatoes, green beans, and homemade rolls. I hadn't told anyone else besides Barb about the Jay-Hank fiasco; I hadn't even had the heart to call Linda. For someone with a detective's mind, she certainly made a mistake as far as this whole mystery was concerned!

"That was some job you did on Jay Thompson's horse, Mattie," commented Dad as he helped himself to more potatoes. He chuckled. "With you around it looks like I'm going to have to stay on my toes. The way that boy raved about you—"

"Jay?" I could feel the tips of my ears burning. I hoped Nita, who was sitting next to me, wouldn't notice. She'd never let me off the hook until I told her the whole gruesome story.

"He said he goes to school with you," my father chattered on, unconscious of the way the conversation was affecting me. "Seemed like a nice boy. I don't think I've heard you mention him, but he certainly seemed to think a lot of you."

"Oh, you know Mattie," said Nita, stuffing in a forkful of green beans. "She has *tons* of secret admirers. So many she can't keep track of them all. Though I don't know why she'd want to keep Jay Thompson a secret. He's *cute*. A ten and a half in my opinion."

"Too bad your opinion doesn't count," I shot back. That was one night I wasn't in the mood for Nita's sarcastic sense of humor.

"Now, girls," Dad warned, giving us his sternest look, which was about as threatening as a bear cub's. "You know the rules. No fighting at the dinner table."

"OK," Nita whispered. "We'll make up for it later on in our room. I challenge you to a duel with pillows."

Zac banged on his high chair in delight, crowing at the top of his lungs. No one could tell him to shut up.

The phone rang.

I dropped my fork, and it clattered to my plate with what seemed a deafening noise. I could feel myself turning red. Suddenly everyone at the table was looking at me.

"Were you expecting a call, Mattie?" asked my father.

"Uh—no." I swallowed hard, forcing down the lump of potatoes that was stuck in my throat. I stood up. "I'll go see who it is."

I caught it on the fourth ring. It was only Linda. Had I been hoping it was Jay?

"Oh—hi," I said.

"Hi, yourself. You sound disappointed. Who did you think it would be?"

"Nobody in particular," I lied. "What's up?"

"I just called to tell you the latest news— Curt and Sueann are back together again."

"That's great," I said distractedly.

"You don't sound too excited about it."

"Well, Curt and Sueann break up at least once a month."

"I just thought you might be *vaguely* interested."

"I am. It's just that—" I lowered my voice so no one else would hear. "I've got other things on my mind right now."

"What things? Did Hank call?"

"Not exactly." I told her all about the afternoon, about Jay. I was surprisingly calm about the whole thing, considering the hysterics I'd gone through earlier.

Linda wasn't calm. "That's awful!" she said. "What are you going to do?"

"I don't know."

She was silent for a moment, then she said, "You know something, I didn't want to tell you this before, but I never really thought Hank was right for you. He just didn't seem your type."

"I guess this proves you were right."

"I'm sorry, Mattie."

"About what?"

"About Hank—what else? You must be brokenhearted!"

127

Actually, I was thinking more about Jay than Hank. I realized that the reason I'd been more angry with Jay was that I felt more betrayed by him. *He* was the one I'd opened up to, not Hank. Jay was the one who said he loved me. . . .

I wondered if he had really meant it.

"I think you were right about Hank," I said. "He wasn't really my type. I *wanted* him to be, so I guess I let myself believe he was everything I'd ever dreamed of. Sort of like those connect-the-dots puzzles we used to do when we were kids. Maybe if I hadn't been so dreamy-eyed, I would've figured it out about Jay before now."

"Then you're not in love with him anymore?"

"I don't think I ever really was."

"What about Jay?"

"What *about* him?"

"Are you in love with him?" She practically screamed the question at me.

"How should I know? I barely know him."

As soon as I'd said it, though, I knew it wasn't true. In some ways, I probably knew Jay a lot better than I'd ever known Hank.

"I can't believe it," Linda said. "I spend my whole life thinking up mysteries, and here was the biggest mystery of all happening right under my nose, and I didn't even know it." She sighed. "Promise me something. Don't tell anyone about this, or my reputation may be ruined for good."

"Don't worry! My lips are sealed."

"Listen, Mattie," she advised. "Don't let this get you down, no matter what. I have a feeling it'll all work out for the best."

It was the second time that day that someone had told me that. People are always saying things like that just to make you feel better. The truth is, things *don't* always work out for the best—or they take so long to work out that by the time you get there, you forget why it mattered in the first place. I remember my mother telling me that about the divorce. Eventually, I suppose, it did work out for the best, but what good did it do me at the time?

The phone rang again that night just as I was brushing my teeth. Nita was at a friend's overnight, and I had offered to sit for Zac, who had actually gone to sleep with no problem. Since I wasn't expecting any calls, I didn't rush to answer the phone. I picked it up on the fifth ring.

"Hi," Jay said. "I almost hung up. I figured no one was home."

"I'm here," I said. Why is it we always say the dumbest things at the most important moments of our lives?

"Are you going to hang up on me now that you know who it is?" he asked. His voice was no longer a husky growl, but it still sent tingles up the back of my neck.

The last bit of my anger dissolved into a little laugh. "I should, shouldn't I? What you did was—"

"Disgusting, despicable, dishonest," he supplied readily. "I know, I know. Don't think there's a name I haven't already called myself."

"I may think of a few more. Give me time."

"How about irresistible?"

"Definitely not," I said, aware that I was thawing faster than I'd intended.

"You mean you can resist going out with me next Saturday?" he asked teasingly.

"I haven't forgiven you yet," I said, stalling.

"OK," he said. "You have exactly one week to go on hating me. Then I'll pick you up at eight on Saturday."

"You have a lot of nerve," I told him.

"Yeah, I know. That's what got me into so much trouble, remember?"

"How could I forget!"

"So will you go out with me?"

"I don't know. I thought you were dating Janine. Won't she be jealous?"

"Janine and I are just friends," he explained. "Actually, if you want to know the truth, she had her eye on Hank the whole time. She's had a crush on him since way back when."

It didn't surprise me. Nothing would ever surprise me again. Not after this. I didn't doubt that Linda would become the next Agatha Christie or that Nita would someday land on the cover of *Cosmopolitan*. I didn't think I'd be surprised if Hank wrote me after this, saying he'd actually *met* King Kong up on the Empire State Building. I'd probably even tell him to say hello for me.

"What do you say?" Jay urged. "Will you give me another chance?"

I thought for a minute, then smiled. "How do I know this is *really* Jay?"

"Give me a chance, and I'll prove it. Only not over the phone," he murmured. "From now on, I'm going to do all my proving in person."

Somehow, I had a feeling he would.

Sweet Dreams

We hope you enjoyed reading this book. All the titles currently available in the Sweet Dreams series are listed on the next two pages. They are all available at your local bookshop or newsagent, though should you find any difficulty in obtaining the books you would like, you can order direct from the publisher, at the address below. Also, if you would like to know more about the series, or would simply like to tell us what you think of the series, write to:

Kim Prior,
Sweet Dreams.
Transworld Publishers Limited,
Century House,
61-63 Uxbridge Road,
London W5 5SA.

To order books, please list the title(s) you would like, and send together with your name and address, and a cheque or postal order made payable to TRANS-WORLD PUBLISHERS LIMITED. Please allow cost of book(s) plus 20p for the first book and 10p for each additional book for postage and packing.

Dear SWEET DREAMS reader,

Since we started publishing SWEET DREAMS almost two years ago, we have received hundreds of letters telling us how much you like the series and asking for details about the books and the authors.

We are getting to know quite a lot about our readers by now and we think that many of you would like a club of your own. That's why we're setting up THE SWEET DREAMS CLUB.

If you would like to become a member, just fill in the details below and send it to me together with a cheque or postal order for £1.50 (payable to The Sweet Dreams Club) to cover the cost of our postage and administration. Your membership package will contain a special SWEET DREAMS membership card, and a SWEET DREAMER newsletter packed full of information about the books and authors, beauty tips, a fascinating quiz and lots more besides (including a fabulous special offer!).

Now fill in the coupon (in block capitals please), and send, with payment, to:

The Sweet Dreams Club,
Freepost (PAM 2876),
London W5 5BR.

N.B. No stamp required.

I would like to join the Sweet Dreams Club.

Name:...

Address:..

...

I enclose a cheque/postal order for £1.50, made payable to The Sweet Dreams Club.